Liv gripped the counter behind her. "I can't go anywhere with you. We hate each other, remember?"

Alexander laughed, the rippling sound of it surrounding her in overwhelming waves. "Yes, but not as much as I hate being front-page fodder for trashy tabloids."

"This isn't funny." She moved away from the intoxicating scent of the dratted man. "I have to do a pitch for our agency in two weeks. I can't miss it."

"Still playing at being the hardworking career woman? Give it up, Olivia. You don't have it in you."

She pushed out the fury scratching at her throat and steadied herself. "It's your honeymoon, Alexander. No one will know you're by yourself unless you advertise it."

His fingers gripped her arm and turned her around, his gaze frantic in its search of hers. "You truly live in your own world, don't you?" Bitterness laced his every word. "The press hounds me wherever I go, whatever I do, and I refuse to throw even a morsel of scandal their way. If you're not going to tell me the truth, you're damn well going to stick with me until Kim's back."

The Sensational Stanton Sisters

Notoriety has a new name!

The exploits of the famous, or should that be *in*famous, Stanton Sisters are guaranteed to sell newspapers the world over.

While they are physically identical, the sisters are as different as night and day.

Olivia Stanton can create scandal from thin air, but this bad girl is desperate to be oh-so-good. Until she comes face-to-face with the one man whose dark looks are a temptation too far!

Kimberly Stanton is the stunning socialite with a brilliant head for business. But when her dirty little secret comes back to haunt her, Kim's entire life is turned upside down!

One thing's for sure—both deserve the middle name "trouble" with a capital *T!*

And what of the men sent to tame them?

We wish them luck!

This month, read Tara Pammi's stunning debut in:

A Hint of Scandal

October 2013

Next month, read Kimberly Stanton's story in:

A Touch of Temptation

November 2013

Tara Pammi

—

A Hint of Scandal

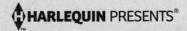

Recycling programs
for this product may
not exist in your area.

ISBN-13: 978-0-373-13190-7

A HINT OF SCANDAL

Copyright © 2013 by Tara Pammi

Printed in U.S.A.

All about the author...
Tara Pammi

TARA PAMMI can't remember a moment when she wasn't lost in a book—especially a Harlequin romance novel, which provided so much more excitement to a teenager than a mathematics textbook. It was only years later, while struggling with her two-hundred-page thesis in a basement lab, that Tara realized what she really wanted to do—write a romance novel. She already had the requirements—a wild imagination, and a love for the written word.

Tara lives in Colorado with the most cooperative man on the planet and two daughters. Her husband and daughters are the only things that stand between Tara and a full-blown hermit life with only books for company.

Tara would love to hear from readers. She can be reached at tara.pammi@gmail.com or through her website, tarapammi.com.

This is Tara's stunning debut—we hope you love it as much as we do!

Did you know this is also available as an ebook?

For my real-life hero—my husband, Raghu, for being my biggest supporter, my strength and the wind beneath my writing wings.

For the Minxes of Romance—for being the most generous and awesome online family I could ever ask for.

For my editor, Pippa, for her incredible patience and invaluable advice—this wouldn't have been possible without you.

CHAPTER ONE

"KIMBERLY, DO YOU take this man, Alexander King, to be your lawfully wedded husband, until death do you part?"

Nooooo.

Olivia Stanton looked around in alarm. *Had she said it aloud?* Her fingers slipped on the satin ribbon that held the elaborate orchid and white rose bouquet in her hand. Her heart pounded. The calm, bespectacled priest looked back at her patiently. She released the breath she'd been holding and pulled another one in. The scent of the flowers in her hand enveloped her, the sweet smell intensifying her panic.

Seconds ticked by. The silent anticipation of the guests behind was her a tidal wave threatening to pull her under.

Her gaze collided with Alexander King's: blue, cool and unflappable. His composure in the face of her anxiety grated on her already-taut nerves. Her tongue stuck to the roof of her mouth. Her heart roared in her ears, a thundering beat in contrast to the silence enclosing them.

She couldn't do this. Yes, they had done it before, Kim and she—pretended to be each other. Usually Kim pretended to be Liv, to save her from getting into trouble with their father, with the school authorities. So she owed it to Kim. Her successful, accomplished twin had saved her ass more times than Liv could count.

But to marry Alexander King in her place… An extreme step even for her.

"I can't marry him today. I'll be back soon."

Her twin's words rang in her ears. If Kim, who was ever dependable and unwavering, had to leave at the last minute, in a panic, surely it had to be something serious. Wouldn't Alexander understand if she pulled him aside and explained everything?

"Don't tell Alex. He'll be disappointed in me. He despises even a hint of scandal."

What kind of a man was her twin involved with if she couldn't confide in him over her doubts on the most important day of their lives?

A hand at her elbow, the touch infinitely gentle, pulled her back into the waking nightmare. She tilted her head. Alexander's blue gaze trapped hers, shooting questions she wasn't equipped to answer. Yet his gaze was gentle. He must care for her sister, for she had never spied a trace of tenderness in him before. Because even in the very little time she had spent with her sister's successful, intensely private fiancé, Olivia had realized that Alexander King hated her guts.

"I don't want to lose him."

Kim's desperate plea pumped blood back into her numb brain. Ungluing her tongue from the roof of her mouth, Olivia took a deep breath and uttered the scariest words of her life. "I do."

His face settling into benevolent lines, the priest relaxed. "I pronounce you husband and wife. You may now kiss the bride."

The bottom dropped out from under her. Alexander's hands on her bare shoulders sent sparks of raw sensation zinging through her. He pulled her closer as she fought the awareness spreading to every inch of her. The scent of his soap and skin seeped into the air she breathed. The pad of his thumb felt rough against the sensitive skin of her cheek.

He was going to kiss her. Olivia couldn't move. The truth dawning on her was immobilizing her thought processes. Only one thing flared inside her mind like a gaudy neon sign. She wanted nothing more than to sink into his kiss.

He bent his mouth toward her and her heart pumped harder and faster. His breath mingled with hers and unbearable longing consumed her. It was too much to fight. More than she could resist.

No.

Mere seconds before his mouth touched her lips she turned her head, anchoring her hands on his chest. His mouth landed at the corner of hers, his lips soft and firm at the same time.

Heat blasted through her everywhere, inside and out. From where his mouth touched her. From his all-too-possessive hands on her hips. And an overpowering need that she couldn't misinterpret. *What was the matter with her?*

His blue gaze seared hers, curiosity and awareness shooting out at her from its bright depths. His grip on her waist tightened as he pulled her to him. The solid wall of his body was a taste of heaven against her curves. Not succumbing to the temptation of his kiss was the hardest thing she had ever done in her life.

She fought the groan rising through her. *This was all she needed.* A pithy curse fell from her lips. His head tilted toward her as if he had heard it. Her chest constricted with fear, the corset of the intricate designer dress cutting off her breath.

Alexander King was nothing if not astute and ruthless. How long before he discovered her deception?

Alexander King studied his wife's face, alarm bells ringing inside his head. The rapid beat of the pulse at her neck, the restless way she shied away from making eye contact with anyone, the way she had sidled away from his kiss. *Something wasn't right.*

As though aware of his continued scrutiny, her brown gaze flew to his and then moved away. Something was different about her.

He had felt it the moment she had come to a halt next to him. Instead of meeting his eyes, even then she had seemed cagey. It wasn't just that the poised composure and the quiet, unassuming grace that were so much a part of her were missing. There was an edge to her every movement, a defiant tilt to her chin. Even now she fidgeted with the diamond choker at her throat, her teeth clamped on her lower lip. As though the necklace was strangling her.

Then there was the way she looked. Not that he hadn't expected Kim to look beautiful. Just that he hadn't expected her to look so...*erotic* in her wedding dress. What he would have expected to be understated elegance instead looked earthily sexy, right down to the bloodred lipstick— something he had never seen her wear before.

The sight of her white teeth tugging at the luscious curve of her mouth sent a stab of fierce lust coursing through him. He had been attracted to her before, of course. But it had been nothing like the blaze of need sweeping through him, tightening his lower body.

He wanted to bury his mouth in the crook of her neck, where her pulse hammered. The ivory-colored dress cupped her breasts like a lover every time she drew breath, daring him to replace its hold with his hands. A tiny birthmark on the slope of her breast cried out for his touch.

He stole a hand around her waist and pulled her to the side, away from his cheering friends. She instantly stiffened against him like a coiled spring. *Tense, unyielding.* He bent his head, a smile in place. Something earthy and floral assaulted his nostrils. He closed his eyes and fought for control over his libido. His hands tightened around her waist, pulling her closer to breathe in more of her delicious scent.

He frowned, trying to think clearly through the lust clouding him. What was so different today from the past six months? He'd had no problem taking it slow, as she had requested, whereas today he couldn't wait to get her into bed.

"Is everything okay, Kim?"

Looking somewhere near his shoulder, she smiled. The false brightness of her smile notched up his doubts a little more.

"Yes, thank you, Alexander." With a subtle movement, she slipped out of the crook of his arm. "I think the stress of the past few weeks has caught up with me."

A vague suspicion slithered in his gut. Something stirred just under the surface but he couldn't put his finger on it. "Alexander?"

Color blasted into her cheeks and for the second time in the past hour he heard a curse fall from her lips. A minute's regret slashed through him. There were blue shadows under her eyes. Her skin was drawn too tight over her features.

He prided himself on not missing the tiniest detail. Yet he had completely overlooked that she was tired. After all, she had singlehandedly planned the wedding, without a trace of anxiety and with minimum input from him.

Not only was she successful and sophisticated, she had an unblemished reputation, the respectability he needed in a wife and—the best part—she was the perfect role model for his sister. The increasing restlessness and unhappiness he had spied in Emily, the rumors floating around about his mother, meant he'd needed a wife and soon. Kim was the perfect solution.

Her hands went to her forehead, her long fingers rubbing at her temples. "I'm sorry. I'm just a little tired."

"You organized everything brilliantly, Kim. Everything went smoothly, without a ripple." He ran his finger over the inside of her wrist. "Perfect. Just like you."

Her chocolate-brown eyes widened and her luscious red mouth pinched into a thin line. "Yeah, it looks beautiful." She glanced around them once again, disbelief flickering in her face. "Thanks, I mean."

As the photographer arranged the wedding party around the entrance the missing piece clicked in his head. He looked around, searching for the pale pink outfits that indicated the bridesmaids. *Of course. Olivia was missing.* He should have known the reason Kim was upset. Everything else she had planned had gone so perfectly.

"Where's Olivia?"

"She…had to leave." Kim shrugged, her stiff shoulders betraying her. "Something urgent came up."

Irritation flickered through him. Olivia was nothing if not predictable when it came to being selfish and irresponsible. Yet Kim seemed surprised at every turn by her reckless twin. "I should have known it would be something to do with *her.* What has she done now?"

Her chin tilted up, her mouth narrowing into a stubborn line. Liquid fire flashed in her chocolate gaze, her withdrawal immediate. "Olivia didn't do anything."

The one point of contention between Kim and him. Her attachment to her selfish, troublemaking twin was beyond his understanding. He smoothed out the ire rising through him. "She always hurts you, Kim. Isn't it time to cut her out of your life like your father did?"

Olivia stared at him, aghast, her palms fisting at her sides. She couldn't believe the arrogance of the man. *He was encouraging her sister to cut her off—the one person who cared about her.* Her throat burned with anger.

Anger that she couldn't let out. What had Kim seen in this man? She glared at him. "She's my sister. I won't cut off my family as ruthlessly as you have just because they're not perfect."

His shoulders tightened under the handmade Italian tuxedo. His jaw tensed into a tight line. The forcefield of his anger encompassed her, drowning out the sounds around them.

Olivia braced herself, ready for his outrage to burst and choke her. After all, she had faced it countless times with her father. She had always frozen when the hurricane of her father's anger had burst. It was Kim who'd been the wall of steel that had saved her. Shame coursed through her. And here she was, mouthing off again and ruining Kim's chance with Alexander.

But the outburst she had expected didn't come. Instead, he smiled, his anger obviously under control. The lethal smile wrapped itself around her senses, almost successful in making her forget what had made her so mad to begin with.

"I provoked you," he said with a crease in his brow, as if he was contemplating her.

His asinine control grated on her nerves. She would have liked to see him blow his top. Then she would have had a measure of him. Instead, he had turned the tables on her, making her feel she should apologize instead. She did it, anyway. For Kim, she reminded herself for the nth time. "I'm sorry," she said, uncaring that she didn't sound sorry in the least.

The click of a camera brought her head up just as Alexander's arms enfolded her. She took a quick peek at the silver Rolex on his strong wrist. The metal shone on his brown skin, a contrast to the crystal blue of his eyes. He was an interesting study in genetics, with his Nordic father and Italian mother. If only it was her interest in genetics that had her heart drumming like a heavy metal rock band.

Only two hours had passed since Kim had left and this day already felt too long. She held herself rigid in his arms, her neck and shoulders aching at the pressure to stay still and not lean back into his corded strength.

His hands settled on the curve of her hips. Her cheek rubbed against his rougher one. Her breasts felt heavy, tight, and a throbbing in her lower belly shot its way between her legs. *Arousal.* Damn, the man was to be her sister's husband. *Eventually.* She closed her eyes and thought of Kim—the happiness in her face at their engagement, the sparkle in her tone whenever she had spoken of Alexander. It helped dampen the rush of sensation settling over her. Even if only a little.

She tilted her head to the side, ready to beg him to let her go. Instead, their eyes locked and she found herself caught.

"Relax, Kim. Remember this is supposed to be the biggest day of your life."

Olivia gripped the marble countertop in the exquisite bath in Kim's suite, everything within her rebelling at the idea of walking back into the banquet hall. It was a temporary respite before the reception began and she never wanted it to end.

To hell with the reception and the guests.

The expansive bathroom, with its perfectly placed sconces and chandeliers, the cool Turkish limestone tiles, was more than welcoming. She played with the idea of hiding out right there.

But hiding here would mean drawing Alexander's attention to her.

Her gut flipped at the thought.

She sprinkled cold water on her wrists and face, careful not to spoil her makeup. She wanted to scrub the whole lot off. But Kim always looked perfect and she wasn't going to quicken Alexander's race to the truth that the wrong twin—the *imperfect* one—had stood next to him and uttered vows. At least Kim had promised to be back by nightfall.

She stared into the gold-edged mirror, still unable to believe how different, how polished she looked. Her wild mass of golden-brown curls had been ironed into submission and set into a stylish chignon at the back of her neck. Her neck shone with an elegant diamond choker set in white gold—which she knew was a wedding gift from Alexander *Perfect* King—instead of her mother's heart-shaped locket on a black string, and her feet ached from the four-inch-heeled Christian Louboutin sandals that had already caused untold damage to her back. She scrunched her nose at Kim's makeup bag, where the tube of pink gloss was winking at her. Olivia Stanton in shiny pink lip-gloss was never going to happen. She could only go so far, even for her twin.

She reapplied her dark red lipstick. *Battle-ready.*

She took a deep breath, stepped out of the luxurious suite and walked toward the huge banquet hall. Almost at the entrance, she let her gaze fell on a small veranda to her right, and before she knew it she was looking at miles of gorgeous sand, her feet itching to feel the grainy texture.

With a sigh, she took an about-turn, determined to go for a swim by the end of the day. What was the fun in getting fake married on a Caribbean island if you didn't even dip your toes in the ocean?

She came to a standstill at the entrance to the hall, stunned by the sight. A lump lodged in her throat at the elegant beauty of the hall. Kim had prepared all this for her beautiful wedding and wasn't even here to enjoy it. A hundred little questions pecked inside her head. By the end of this charade she was going to ensure one thing. She'd find out what was really going on with Kim.

Round tables covered with the sheerest white lace filled the decadent marble-floored hall, with a single pink orchid in a crystal vase gracing the center of each table. Lanterns designed to look like tiny fireflies hung from the roof, throwing light onto the vases, and the crystal shimmered in thousands of directions.

It all looked gloriously romantic even to someone like her, who didn't go for the elaborate traditional wedding, the designer gown and the whole status thing that went with the society that Kim and Alexander inhabited.

She couldn't stop her thoughts from flitting inward. Her chest felt tight, as if a fist had tightened over her heart. One more thing Kim had that she herself never would. *A man who loved her. A man who...*

Enough.

She wasn't going to spend another minute thinking about things that could never be. She ran a hand over her stomach and smoothed the silk, feeling as though the hole she kept carefully covered was exposed. She headed straight to the open bar, uncaring of the curious glances thrown her way. Thankfully, the bar itself was empty. She ordered a scotch, her back to everyone. When the drink came she drank it in one swig, needing the fiery liquid to wash away the maudlin nonsense in her head.

Her skin prickled with awareness, every inch of her hypersensitive to the arrival of the man behind her.

"Here's where you're hiding."

Without turning around she silently slid the tumbler back toward the bartender. Kim couldn't stomach alcohol— much less scotch—a fact she was sure Alexander knew. Schooling her face into a pleasant expression, she turned around. The sight of him dealt her a fiercer kick than the scotch. "More like recuperating," she replied, placing her hand in his outstretched one.

He tugged her close, his gaze devouring her. A frown creased his forehead. "Did you just have a drink?"

Managing to hold on to another curse by biting the inside of her cheek, Olivia shook her head.

His disbelief hung like a curtain between them. Instantly she tried to remedy her mistake. "I actually took some aspirin for my headache. It just seems to be getting worse." At least *that* wasn't a lie. Her head was beginning to throb as though she had spent all night at a Metallica concert. In the front row.

His brow cleared and his gaze shone with sympathy. "At least no one will find it strange if we escape the reception quickly. After all, it's our wedding night."

Her gaze flew to his as he ran a long, dark finger over the sensitized flesh at her neck, tracing the lacy neckline of her dress. Her soft gasp got lost between them as he bent toward her ear.

"I can't wait to rip that dress off you."

A shiver traveled up her spine, sparking desire in every inch of her. Locking arms with him, she tucked her head down, fighting for air. His muscled body only heightened her awareness of him. Every second that passed was twisting the hard knot in her stomach tighter. *Where the hell was Kim?* She didn't want to be here for another minute, not with the way her body was reacting to his mere presence.

Not when it was another woman's man. Dear God, he belonged to her twin—the one person who had stood by her no matter what.

Somehow Olivia held on to a semblance of composure as she smiled and talked to the guests, nodding enthusiastically as Kim and Alexander's friends raved on and on and about how perfect they were for each other, pretending to know them. If they thought it was strange that the always intelligent and articulate Kim was mostly silent, they could put it down to the excitement of being a new bride.

She had to bite the inside of her mouth to stop thrusting her tongue out as her father praised Kim's success to anyone who would hear… If only he knew…

She had no idea how she lived through the torturous dance with Alexander. Each sinuous, slow movement threw her against his muscled strength, with the pulsating energy between them winding her up, the scent of him seeping into her every pore. Her muscles groaned at her stiff posture by the time the dance came to an end. Only the enticing prospect of sinking into the claw-foot bathtub with numerous silver faucets she had spied back in Kim's suite kept her standing.

Just as she released a breath of relief and untangled herself from Alexander the front man of the lively native band announced the bride's dance with her father.

No, no, no.

Olivia froze midway on the polished lacquer floor, feeling the color leach out of her face. Fear gripped her insides in an unforgiving knot, and the corseted bodice of her gown was crushing her lungs as her father walked toward her, a genial smile on his handsome face, the very image of a loving father, his stride purposeful as ever.

She couldn't do this. She couldn't dance with him—not without the whole pretense blowing up in her face. She shivered, sliding into the skin of that clumsy fifteen-year-old forced to dance with her father on her birthday. *Stand up tall and look me in the eye.* She could still hear the caustic hiss of his disapproval when she had accidentally trod on his toe, could still feel the painful, cutting press of his fingers on the skin of her shoulders, eroding another piece of her.

The more he criticized, the more she had faltered. He

would have gone on forever except Kim had intervened, claiming her turn, and proceeded to pacify him with her perfection. *Always*. Kim had done it to divert their father's attention from her. Liv knew that. But in the end her twin's perfection had only showcased Olivia's failure even more.

The memory coursed through her like acid, eating away at the armor she had grown, exposing wounds that she had thought covered, if not healed. She gasped for breath when a guest stopped her father. She hadn't talked to him in six years and she couldn't now. He would know in a nanosecond that she wasn't Kim. And he wouldn't even go along with it until she could explain. No, he would bring holy hell down upon her right there, until the whole world gleefully concluded that Olivia Stanton had once again screwed up—and this time her own sister's life.

Pain sliced through her, robbing her of breath. The very intensity of it was still so raw. She wanted to be able to look him in the eye, not to flinch when she saw the corroding disappointment in his gaze. But she couldn't, because nothing had changed. She just wasn't good enough—not now, not ever. Not even to be a stand-in for her perfect sister.

She rubbed her forehead with trembling hands and turned toward the exit, her legs rubbery. "My head feels awful. Please apologize to my father," she threw at Alexander.

She could feel his razor-sharp gaze drill into her back until she stepped out of the banquet hall. But she couldn't look back. Right now, all she needed was to escape.

Picking up a champagne flute from a passing waiter, Alexander stilled and stared at Kim's retreating form. She looked pale and intensely troubled, her hurried gait anything but graceful. And even as he watched she tottered on those heels. The doubts that had been niggling at him all evening crystallized into irrefutable truth, shock stunting his movements.

The woman running away as though the devil was on her heels was Olivia Stanton, the embodiment of everything he despised in a woman—selfish, impulsive and scandalous—who could wreck everything: his reputation, his sister's care. With one reckless word or action.

Kim would have never run at the sight of her father. No, it was Olivia who couldn't run fast enough. After all, the rift between Jeremiah Stanton and his younger daughter was continuing fodder for the tabloids, among other things.

Fury washed up through him in tidal waves, an incessant drumbeat drowning out the innocent chatter around him. *Why had they switched? When had they switched?*

The answer came to him with crushing clarity. He had slipped the wedding ring onto Olivia's finger, his gaze snagging on her lips, fascinated by the blood-red lipstick, wondering how he had missed this side of a woman he had known for six months.

Everything he had worked for his entire life now rested in the hands of a good-for-nothing party girl who didn't know the meaning of responsibility.

The crack of the champagne flute in his hand pulled him out of the red mist. Ignoring Jeremiah's concern, he took a turn toward the exit.

He made his way to the suite that Kim had occupied since her arrival at his mansion a week ago, his steps unhurried in contrast to the blistering anger coursing through him.

Olivia was going to rue the day her self-centered, worthless existence had entered his life.

CHAPTER TWO

HAVING NOT FOUND her in the suite, he'd looked out at the beach view. Something white and gossamer shimmered in the moonlight, contrasting against the dark backdrop of the ocean.

His heart racing, Alexander quickened his steps over the landscaped wooden floor. The minuscule light thrown by the artistically placed lanterns along the gravel path did nothing to make his mounting fury abate. Disbelief poured through him, stalling his usually quick thought processes. He hurried past the artificial landscape, reaching the untouched strip of beach behind the mansion that was his private haven.

He came to a standstill, his heart pounding. Used to the pitch-dark of the night, he turned his head in time to see a flash of alabaster skin, a pale shoulder above the powerful waves. She was about half a mile ahead, and even in the moonlight he could see that she was struggling, her strokes not very elegant or even strong.

The wedding dress and the silver sandals lay in a pile on the sand. The rip in the lacy neckline was visible even in the limited light, a testament to the rush she had been in. The custom-made diamond necklace, his wedding gift to Kim, glittered on top of the lace.

He glanced around the beach he knew like the back

of his hand. Miles of sand and ocean stretched on either side. There would be no one around except his security men at the far end of the estate. No guest was allowed to venture into this private strip. She could drown and no one would know.

His hands fisted at his sides. Olivia Stanton gave new meaning to recklessness. Undoubtedly Kim was somewhere cleaning up her mess while Olivia lazed around in the aftermath of her upheaval. Only she had messed with the wrong man this time. Someone should have taught the selfish woman a lesson a long time ago.

Alex settled down on a lounger, his anger under control and something more insidious crawling into its place. Just how far was the wild Olivia willing to take her pretense?

Olivia sucked in a greedy breath as another wave sluiced over her, pushing her back a little more. She wanted to linger in the water, but her shoulders and arms were beginning to hurt. She had never been the greatest swimmer, but the cold water had pierced through the bubble of anguish that had swathed her, choked her. The dark silence of the moonlit night had been a diversion—at least for a few minutes.

She grunted and pushed through the water at a pace that had her arms feeling like lead weights, her thighs groaning at the exertion. She was always going to be a coward when it came to her father, never daring to stand up to him. She would always run instead.

She reached the sand with a guttural groan, her limbs feeling like rubber. She lay facedown, her lungs a deadweight in her chest. Sand stuck to her wet skin and hair, chafing at her. She had narrowly missed her father's wrath but she still had Alexander to deal with. *If Kim didn't return soon.*

Mere seconds after the thought, the hair on her nape stood up, her skin prickling with a panic she couldn't shake off.

"Are you naked?"

The question startled her, laced with a huskiness that gave her goose bumps. She tilted her head up in the direction of the voice. Alexander was sprawled on a lounger half a foot away, an arm flung behind him casually, watching her, his expression hidden by the fan of his lashes.

Yet there was nothing casual about his gleaming blue eyes, or in the calculating appraisal in them as they traveled over her. With his jacket gone and the neck of his white shirt unbuttoned, which exposed a thoroughly distracting strip of brown flesh, he wasn't the hardheaded businessman anymore. Instead, a touch of roguish danger simmered around him.

Olivia swallowed. She had run straight to the beach as if the devil himself were after her, the only thought in her mind to flee. Now he had another point against her. The idea of slipping back into the water with the possibility of sinking like a stone held more allure than facing him.

She sat up slowly and scrunched her knees to her chest. Pretending to be brushing off the sand on her legs, she gripped them, waiting for the shaking to subside. Refusing to look at him, she stared straight ahead, the tranquility she had found earlier evaporating like a mist. Her fingers slipped on her legs as he moved closer and came to a standstill near her.

She gave up the fight and turned. His feet were coming into her view. Nothing there that would make her feel even a little better—like a lot of hair on the toes or a couple of unsightly growths. No, instead, they were large brown feet, with evenly spaced toes. *"You know what they say about men with large feet, Olivia."* Her friend Amelie's declaration skated into her head and she grinned.

Not now, Liv. "Of course I'm not naked." *Why did she*

sound so unsteady? Dusting away the remnants of sand, she stood up, still not meeting his eyes. "I need a shower."

With a small movement he shifted his body to block hers. His fingers settled on her bare shoulders.

Liv shivered, the hot press of his fingers searing her skin. "Alexander—"

His finger moved to her mouth, effectively silencing her. "You robbed me of the pleasure of ripping that dress off you. At least let me look at what I would have discovered."

Her tummy took a roll as he took a step back. *Look away, Liv.* Through sheer willpower she resisted the temptation to meet his gaze. Only that was worse. With her eyes closed every other sense became hyperaware. Her ears tuned in to the sound of his fractured breathing, her nose was filled with the scent of sea and male arousal, and her skin tingled as though he'd run his hands all over her.

Alex couldn't take his eyes off her body. Heat surged through him, tautening his lower belly. His blood was flowing hotter and faster, making a beeline to regions south. He hadn't asked the question to be censorious. He had been genuinely curious. She had surfaced out of the water and had lain there, the whoosh of her uneven breathing puncturing the silence all around. Her alabaster skin shimmered in the moonlight. The dip of her back and the curve of her butt sent a swift kick of lust to his groin.

Now he understood. She wore nude-colored underwear. At this close distance it was quite modest, compared to the lacy underwear flaunted in every fashion magazine. But then, those lacy, gossamer bras and thongs left nothing to the man's imagination.

She looked earthily sexy. Her wild brown hair was tinted with shades of gold. Her breasts rose and fell with her shallow breathing. The sight of her taut nipples behind the thin fabric made his throat dry up. The dip of her waist, the curve of her hips, her toned legs—every inch of her body was an invitation of pleasure, would drive even the most sensible man to distraction.

Color suffused her cheeks at his continued scrutiny. "You're staring at me."

He hadn't meant to. He didn't want to. But she had a body made for sex. Was that why men lost their minds around her? Weak men, who cracked at the first sign of temptation and then it was just a downward spiral. *Like his father.* The passing thought about his father was enough to cool his desire—more effective than an electric shock.

He took a step back, his senses still reeling. "You're an awful swimmer."

Her chin lifted. An imperceptible movement both defiant and hurt.

"If you had drowned no one would even have heard you."

Olivia felt heat creeping up her cheeks. The strong tide had been the reason she had finally waded out. She couldn't admit that to him, though. Summoning every ounce of her meager willpower, she stayed still. Her fingers twitched for action. Either to push him off or sink her fingers into his tousled hair. "I didn't drown."

A smile spread from his mouth, tugging one corner of it upward, creating a delicious dimple. Sinuous heat slithered through her, pooling toward her groin.

His fingers moved to her nape and pressed gently. "I'm glad."

He was pure sex on legs when he smiled like that, and he knew the power he wielded. But that didn't stop the prickle of sensation that crept up along her skin. His contempt she could handle. His seduction, not so much. She took a step back, away from the warm invitation of all that male heat.

He tugged at her wrist, leaving her no choice but to turn around. "Where are you going?"

She folded her arms against her chest, preparing to do her best to sound like her twin. Doubly hard when her heart was galloping in her chest. All she needed was to get away from here—now. Then she would lock herself up until morning. Not that she was scared of him. It was her own aching need, her utter lack of control that she didn't trust. "I would like to sleep alone tonight." She fluttered her eyelashes, praying the man had a decent side. "Please, Alex."

"Fine."

The weight lifted from her shoulders. Before she could think of a response, he pulled her down with him, until they were both sitting down, shoulder to shoulder.

"Kiss me."

Olivia couldn't decide whether to laugh or cry. "But…"

He raised a brow, a mocking smile curving his sexy mouth. "One kiss. You can't deny your husband that."

What woman refused to kiss her husband on her wedding night? But kissing him was tantamount to…

He frowned, his thumb moving over his lush lower lip. It was a deviation in the stark landscape of his face. "You've been acting strange all evening. I'm beginning to wonder—"

She moved toward him, striving hard to ignore the low thrum of anticipation building up inside her. She had no right to kiss the man. Kim had better have a damn good explanation for this charade. Or Alexander would… She didn't even want to contemplate his reaction when he discovered the truth. Goose bumps rose up on her skin, dulling the edge of her desire.

His hands folded across his chest. His gaze devoured her. He was leaving it all to her. With her hands on his forearms she anchored herself and bent forward, making sure no other parts of their bodies touched.

Her eyes flew shut the moment she felt his breath upon her mouth. Tilting her head to the side, she touched her lips to the corner of his mouth, aiming for minimal contact. Every good intention vanished like a puff of smoke as the taste and feel of him singed her. Primal need spiraled through her, leaving a trail of agony in its wake. A groan she couldn't control escaped her. Her hands locked on his chest between them. Their legs were in a tangle. She tucked her head into the crook of his neck, inhaling the wild scent of his arousal, fighting to control her own.

"Say yes," he rasped near her ear.

Oh, how she wanted to find his mouth again with hers, to run her hands all over his corded strength. Swift on the sinful thought's heels guilt shot through her, paralyzing every nerve ending, flushing her with shame from within. Contrary to the fact that the media frequently portrayed her as a poster child for scandal, there was a line Olivia wouldn't cross.

Not again.

She pushed him back with a grunt, frustration and disgust vying within her. "No." She pressed her fingertips into her arms, finding a perverse satisfaction in her painful grip. Trying to regulate her breathing, she offered him a smile. "I mean, not tonight. I'm really tired."

He shot her a hard look, coating the very air between them with a chilly frost. "You taste like scotch and the ocean. And yet Kim can't stand even the smell of alcohol."

She twisted around so quickly that her head spun. His mouth was set into an unforgiving line and his gaze lanced her, the force of his contempt a live wire between them. *He knew it was her.*

She launched at him, outrage giving her much-needed momentum. "You know." His arms between them warded off her blows with little effort. She didn't care. "You know and you still forced me to kiss you. You bastard."

Her words fell off him like waves pushing at the sand. His face hard as granite, he grabbed her wrists. "I wanted to see how far you would go." His mouth tightened and his words were a quiet, menacing whisper. "Color me surprised to discover even *Olivia Stanton* has some morals."

She didn't think. She fisted her hand for a punch. Only his right hand gripped her wrist, his movements quick and agile. She struggled, remembering how hard she had found it to pull herself back from the temptation of his body. And the arrogant jerk had been testing her!

If she hadn't pulled back when she had...if she hadn't found that last ounce of sanity...to think how low she would have fallen....

A sob built inside her. His hands held hers down at either side. He could have easily twisted her arm behind her and hurt her. She wouldn't have blamed him. He didn't. A moan escaped her as he flipped her easily, sandwiching her facedown between the sand and his hard body.

Hating her complete loss of restraint, she wiggled to be free. The silky sand shifted and glided beneath her until his hard body slipped and covered hers in a sinuous whisper that made her mouth dry. His body slammed into her from behind with just enough force to still her.

"Stop it, Olivia."

His breath sounded choppy and disjointed as he raised himself away from her. But it was too late. The incredible caress of his erection against her backside was etched on her body forever.

"I don't want to hurt you."

He already had. Olivia breathed in and out, sand flying into her mouth, hating the gnawing sensation in her stomach. *Why would Alexander King's opinion have the power to hurt her?* She gave that power to no man, not anymore—not since she'd realized she was only asking for more heartache.

She raised her head and turned around. She could do nothing about the trembling in her stomach, but she filled her words with scorn. "I kissed you because I was pretending to be Kim. And, yes, for some unfathomable reason I'm attracted to you. But the whole world knows I've the worst taste in men. What's *your* excuse?"

He didn't have one.

Alexander couldn't remember the last time he had been so aroused, felt so out of tune with his own body. He usually had no problem controlling his needs as it suited him. Yet in that moment he'd had to summon the last ounce of his self-discipline to stay still. Adrenaline pumped through him, begging for release. He sucked a breath in and counted to ten. His muscles burned. He clenched his teeth.

He loosened his grip on her wrists. Her skin was smooth against his fingerpads. Greedily he drank in the luscious temptation she presented. His thighs shook with the need to lean back into her so that he could feel the inviting cradle of her butt against his erection. Desire rattled through him. He moved his fingers up her arm toward the delicate arch of her neck. She gasped. He jerked back as though burned.

What the hell was he doing? He needed to find out where Kim was, get on a flight to Paris... Instead, he...

He moved to his knees and pulled himself away from her, his mind whirring. "What you provoke in me is a physical reaction—purely animalistic. *Temporary insanity* fueled by six months of abstinence. There's nothing more I despise in the world than a man or a woman who can't control those impulses."

As though the fight had left her, she sagged into the ground, careful to move her body away from his. "Please, Alexander. Let me go."

Shifting back, he stared at her, unwilling to touch her even to pull her up.

She sat up and pushed her hair out of her face, her

movements jumpy, her willowy body trembling. His gaze fell to the impressions on her wrists. He sank back to his knees with a silent thud, feeling an invisible punch to his gut. *Dear God, he had done that to her.* Even in the silver light of the moon there was no mistaking the light red marks on her wrists.

Whatever she had done, however much she had provoked him, there was no excuse. Everything he hated within himself, everything he kept tightly bound, had snapped free in a matter of seconds. Shame spiraled through him, cooling his desire, drenching him in a cold sweat—a familiar sick feeling that greeted him like an old friend.

To use brute strength to control…it was the lowest he could sink to.

He pulled her hands into his and cursed when she pulled back like a frightened cat. "We should run some cold water on your wrists."

She stood up, dusting away the sand from her body, her gaze pointedly looking away from him. "I've had worse. This is nothing."

He hated the clawing need to explain that he wasn't that man. But he wouldn't be able to look at himself if he didn't. "You probably don't expect better from the men in your life." He ignored her gasp. "I expect better of myself." He tilted his head, seeking again the proof of his boorish behavior. "I apologize, Olivia. Nothing justifies my behavior."

Her gaze studied him, disbelief pouring out of her stiff shoulders. "I provoked you. I—"

He shook his head. "That's the pathetic excuse of a weak man."

She opened her mouth to argue but he cut her off.

Stepping back from her, he fisted his hands by his side.

"Get dressed. I'll see you inside." His words were clipped, his anger at himself coating his throat. "And don't even think of leaving."

CHAPTER THREE

IF ALEXANDER HAD assumed that he would be less distracted with her dressed, he was wrong. Just as he stepped into the huge open-plan kitchen Olivia entered through the high archway, covered in *his* white robe, the one Kim had borrowed from him two days ago, her honey-gold hair gleaming wet, her skin glowing pink.

He pulled his gaze away from the vee of the robe and poured himself a drink from the bar. The sounds of her puttering around the kitchen beat a tattoo in his head. His patience running dangerously thin, he guzzled down his scotch. The erotic reminder of how it had tasted on *her* was forever imprinted on his mouth.

"I'm waiting, Olivia."

She slammed the door on the state-of-art steel refrigerator and leaned against it. "Is there any chance of finding food in this godforsaken mansion? Or do you expect me to die of hunger?"

He pushed a chair back and sat down, stretched his legs. A slow ache was beginning to build behind his left eye. "Where's Kim?"

She glared at him and started digging around in the numerous cabinets. "I don't know."

"Don't play games with me." He raked a hand through his hair. This morning his life had been mapped out perfectly. He'd been about to marry a woman who was sensible, undemanding—someone who aroused nothing in him except affection and respect, someone who would stand by his side as he gave his sister the life she deserved. Instead, he had slipped the diamond ring on the finger of her antithesis.

"I tend to rebel when threatened—if you don't already know." She poked her head out of the drawer she had been searching and ran a hand through her hair. "Add the fact that my stomach is eating itself, I'm very dangerous right now."

He crossed to her in a minute and cornered her, more annoyed by her presence than Kim's absence. *An irrational reaction if ever he'd had one.* "Don't mistake my patience to be a failing, Olivia." When she tried to turn away, he shifted his body to block her. The scent of her skin surrounded him, assaulting him with images of her in the shower. "Kim was fine this morning. Until you showed up. It's obvious that she's somewhere cleaning up your mess again."

Her mouth opened in protest. She swallowed. The column of her neck drew his gaze. Her hands swept over her stomach. She was nervous and distressed. Finally he was going to get some answers.

"I'm truly hungry, Alexander," she said, her mouth a beguiling pout. "I missed lunch and then ate hardly a morsel at the reception. Can't you order your famous French chef to whip up something? Preferably something substantial."

He fisted his hands, digging deep inside himself for the last scrap of patience. The nerves in his temple stretched taut, as if they would snap at any minute. He pointed her toward the phone on the wall.

With a cheer, she plucked it from the wall and rattled away in French, ordering enough food to feed an army.

He threw her cell phone onto the glass table in between

them, along with the giant metallic silver handbag he'd picked up from Kim's suite. "Call her."

Her eyebrows shot into to her hairline, her molten gaze looking daggers at him. "You went through my things?"

"You stood next to me and pledged to be my wife." He smiled, despite the fact that the situation was slipping out of his control. "Life's a crapshoot."

She tucked the phone into her bag, a frown on her face. "Didn't you see the calls I've been making every fifteen minutes? She's not picking up."

"Then we'll go find her. Tell me where she is."

For the first time this evening she looked anxious. "I don't know. I think she wanted to postpone the wedding but didn't know how to tell you."

She folded her hands and leaned against the gleaming marble counter, a little frown furrowing her brow. He followed her glance to the floor-to-ceiling glass doors leading to the beach and the silence he had always cherished was suffused with tension.

"I don't think she left the island. She said she would be back by now."

"You think this a joke?" He hated the spiraling tension he could feel in himself. He needed to get control of this situation, and if that meant dealing with someone who didn't have a responsible bone in her body, so be it. "Why would Kim walk out at the last minute if it wasn't to deal with whatever mess *you've* gotten yourself into this time?"

Olivia glared at him. "Do you think anything in the world would tempt me to spend time with you other than for my sister? Whether you believe me or not, I did it because Kim asked me to. Now, if you're done blaming me for *helping you,* I would like to get out of here."

"You can't leave." His face settled into a mocking smile. "Even if that sounds very unappreciative of me after all your *help.*"

Sarcastic jerk. "Listen, Alexander. All Kim said was that she couldn't marry you *today.* God knows why."

Olivia felt a tightness around her chest. Her sister hadn't confided in her. Kim had always been the rock between the two of them. It didn't bode well that she'd had to leave on the day of her own wedding. *That was just not...Kim.* Fear for her safety began a rapid tattoo inside Olivia's head. *Where was she?*

"But she still wants you. I mean, she persuaded me into this deception precisely because *she didn't want to lose you*—as she put it."

He didn't bat an eyelid. "If there had been a problem Kim would have come to me—not gone through some elaborate deception and roped *you* in, of all people."

Meaning he had a special dose of contempt reserved just for her? She let his comment pass by, even though his prejudice pricked her. She was used to it now. She was, truly. Yet it still shocked her that people judged her based on her history before spending even an hour with her.

"So, if she had come to you and said that she couldn't marry you tonight it would have been okay? Because she said you would hate even a *hint* of scandal." She should stop there, the oh-so-small sensible part of her warned her. But she had left that part behind years ago. "Not that it really *is* scandalous to postpone a wedding."

"You slapped my friend at my engagement party and made a spectacle of yourself. A man with whom you broke a business contract after he had been decent enough to hire you."

His lush lower lip tapered into a stiff line, hardness entering his blue gaze, and she braced herself.

"Even the word *broke* is too professional for your conduct, because you simply upped and left one day, didn't you? Nothing is scandalous enough for *you,* Olivia."

It wasn't anything she hadn't heard before. But his

scornful words lanced through her and found a vulnerable spot, leaving her shaken to the core.

"Assuming you're telling the truth, *if* Kim had talked to me I would have been married to her—instead of arguing about what constitutes a scandal with *you*."

Olivia took a deep breath, trying hard to suppress the fury rising through her. This wasn't her fight. She couldn't and she *didn't* care what he thought of her. She had done what her sister had asked her to do. Still, his arrogant assumption that Kim would have gone through with the wedding rankled. Didn't he care about Kim's feelings?

Obviously he didn't. Appearances were everything to Alexander King. Even the knowledge that she was in his life for no more than a day couldn't dispel his distaste. And her twin was planning to spend her life with him. She couldn't let him get to her.

"But she *didn't* talk to you. My sister asked me for help and I stepped in. And I look forward to the moment when you know the truth and will grovel at my feet for forgiveness."

Hell would freeze over before Alexander King groveled at her feet. She knew that. But a girl needed her wild fantasies to keep going. It was right up there with making out with Johnny Depp and being able to survive on strawberry martinis. It was better that he'd found her out. She didn't have to pretend to be Kim anymore and could go back to her own life. Far away from *make-one-mistake-and-I'll-cut-you-out* Alexander King.

"So really there's no reason for you and me to stick it out here."

She would have been less shaken by a display of temper in response. But the absolute silence that met her declaration made the hairs on her neck stand up. His broad shoulders blocked everything else. The hint of stubble on his jaw gave him a roguish look. The folded cuffs of his white shirt displayed strong forearms. Her throat dry, she stared back, waiting.

She steeled herself for some scathing remark, but could do nothing about the awareness spreading through her limbs as he loomed over her. He smelled like dark chocolate wrapped in decadent male arousal. If she could bottle the scent she'd be able to sell it without writing a slogan for it. One whiff and women of all ages would be falling over themselves for it.

His finger flicked the tip of her nose, his blue gaze glittering with dark amusement. "You're not suggesting I go on our honeymoon by myself, are you?"

Her smile faltered on her lips, her gut dropping through an endless fall. "You can't be serious," she murmured. His posture screamed unyielding determination, confirming her worst fear. "There's no need. Kim will be back."

"Then you better start hoping she's here tomorrow morning."

She gripped the counter behind her. "I can't go anywhere with you. We hate each other, remember?"

He laughed, the rippling sound of it surrounding her in overwhelming waves. "Yes, but not as much as I hate being front-page fodder for trashy tabloids."

"This isn't funny." She moved away from the intoxicating scent of the dratted man and opened the calendar on her phone. "I have to do a pitch for our agency in two weeks. I can't miss it."

"Still playing at being the hardworking career woman?" His gaze dropped to the sketch pad peeping out of her handbag and dismissed it the next second. "Give it up, Olivia. You don't have it in you."

Her breath whooshed out of her, his words dealing a nasty punch to her middle. Before the phone slipped from her shaky fingers she threw it back into her bag. The pitch to LifeStyle Inc. was the only thing that could build her career—her only opportunity to silence corrosive comments like his. She couldn't miss it. She pushed out the fury scratching at her throat and steadied herself. "It's your honeymoon, Alexander. No one will know you're by yourself unless you advertise it."

His fingers gripped her arm and turned her around. His gaze was frantic in its search of hers. "You truly live in your own world, don't you?" Bitterness laced his every word. "The press hounds me wherever I go, whatever I do, and I refuse to throw even a morsel of scandal their way. If you're not going to tell me the truth, you're damn well going to stick with me until Kim's back."

Unable to control the rising hysteria inside her, Olivia pushed him back with force, every muscle in her flexing with the need to escape. This day couldn't get worse. Was the universe finally catching up with her in the form of this infuriating man?

"Fine. I'll go with you. But I have to return to New York in two weeks. If you try to stop me. If you...." She blew at a lock of hair that fell on her forehead, fighting the urge to pummel him. "Remember, nothing is scandalous enough for me—*and* I have nothing to lose."

"Not even your sister's happiness?"

"I'm seriously beginning to doubt if that lies with *you*." She ran her fingers over her forehead, her head throbbing with increased pressure. "Where are we going?"

He didn't answer. Only stared at her searchingly, his blue gaze inscrutable. And Olivia knew she had been wrong earlier. The day had just gotten much worse—kick-you-while-you're-down worse.

His gaze glittered with unspoken warnings. His mouth was an uncompromising line. "Paris."

Only Olivia Stanton could look like a deer caught in headlights at the mention of Paris.

Alexander stood with his hands folded, his mind whirring, waiting for his staff to finish laying out food on the table. The delicious aromas assailed his nostrils. But even Pierre's culinary talent couldn't entice his hunger tonight. At least not for food.

He should have been in his bed tonight with Kim, lost to the world. Respecting her wishes to take it slow, he hadn't pushed her—which meant he hadn't had sex in six months. Ironic that his libido ran rampant tonight for a woman he didn't even like. He tucked his hands into the pockets of his trousers and turned his head this way and that, trying to loosen the stiffness in his neck muscles.

He turned around as his staff left.

Her face lit up like a child's on Christmas, Olivia was eying the fragrant dishes on the table. Despite himself, he smiled. "I thought you would be too upset to eat?"

Settling down at the dark oak table, she shrugged. "That's your problem."

She bit into a sandwich, slid a little lower in her chair, her head thrown back, and moaned, highlighting the delicate jawline, the graceful arch of her neck. He cursed, feeling too warm in his clothes.

"Like everyone else on the planet, you assume you know me. You don't. For the record, *I am* upset. But it doesn't mean I'll starve myself."

She took a sip of wine and then got up and sauntered over to the intercom again. He watched in fascination as she thanked Pierre in perfect French, a teasing smile coloring her words. She'd probably won over Pierre for life.

Alex moved toward the table, picked up a French fry and popped it into his mouth. He almost missed the look she threw over her shoulder at him. Almost. She was laughing, lounging casually against the wall. But he didn't mistake it for anything other than the show it was.

He couldn't trust Olivia as far as he could throw her

delectable body. She wasn't going to mutely follow orders. He knew it as surely as the tightness he felt in his muscles as she licked her lips and laughed.

He pulled his cell phone out and made a quick call to his head of security, issuing instructions for him to locate Kim. He looked into the darkness, past the French windows, frustration holding him immobile in its grip. With everything he had confided in her Kim should have known better than to leave him with her reckless twin—known there was no way he could travel to Paris without his wife.

He searched through the cabinets and heaped coffee into the state-of-art coffeemaker—the only appliance in the otherwise bare kitchen.

It was going to be a long night. Just not the pleasurable one he'd expected.

He inclined his head when Olivia wished him goodnight and sauntered out of the kitchen.

Until Kim was back he needed the blasted woman—whether he liked it or not.

Olivia tiptoed through the bedroom in the darkness, wary of switching on even the bedside lamp. She pulled on the black cargo-style capris she had left at the foot of the bed last night. The soft material whispered against her skin, the sound of it raising every nerve ending in her to attention in the pitch black of pre-dawn. A mint-green sleeveless top with built-in bra, a white sweatshirt finished her outfit and she pulled on sneakers.

Sliding her laptop and notepad into her handbag, she took one last look around the bedroom. She eyed the suitcase she was leaving behind. Dragging it with her through the silent mansion wasn't an option. Nothing in there that she couldn't replace. She never wanted to lay eyes on that damned designer gown again, anyway. Her stomach growled in hunger. After hearing Alexander's plans for her last night, the delicious food had tasted like sawdust. But she had eaten it, anyway, refusing to let on how much his announcement had derailed her.

Her heart thudding, she opened the door and stepped into the dimly lighted corridor. A feeling of déjà vu descended on her. How many times had she snuck through her high-security private school when she had been a teenager? It hadn't ended well even a single time.

Within minutes she'd entered the main foyer, with the gleaming marble floors that led to several bedrooms. Ceiling lights here and there illuminated her path, drawing attention to the elegant angles of the mansion, shedding light on the priceless art pieces everywhere she looked.

Any other time she would have enjoyed the beauty of this house surrounded by lush gardens and the private beach. Her studio apartment, the size of a walk-in closet, in a not-so-good neighborhood of Manhattan, was hardly conducive to creativity. But this mansion, with its sky-high ceilings taking advantage of natural light during the day, was the perfect location to relax, to let the ideas fighting for life inside her head breathe onto paper.

Except for the pervading presence of the man who owned the mansion, who had no problem rearranging her life to suit *his* plans.

No. She couldn't tolerate another hour in his presence, much less travel with him to Paris, of all places. Just thinking of the city brought a chill to her skin, memories cloying their way to the surface.

Reaching the entrance, she plucked the keys to a Range Rover she had seen in the courtyard from the key-holder. All she needed was to get to the airport, which was fifty miles away, and then get on a flight out of the island. She didn't much care where she went as long as she got out of here in the next couple of hours. The airline ticket was going to max out her credit card, but it was a price she was willing to pay.

She stepped into the wide courtyard, intent on locating the vehicle—and ran headlong into a solid, warm body. Her breath whooshed out of her at the impact, her insides rearranging themselves into jelly.

Alexander.

His hands on her arms anchored her. A dark navy sweater hugged the lean breadth of his chest, and black khakis completed his casual look. His blue, blue eyes shone with razor-edged amusement and he was very much awake. He looked dangerously yummy, and the assault of his clean, fresh scent was too much for her sleep-deprived body.

"Going somewhere, Olivia?"

His smooth words sent prickles of alarm running down her arms. Before she could answer he turned her around and marched her back through the foyer as though she were a petulant teenager.

While he barked orders into his cellphone—no doubt ordering his minions to bar the gates against her—she pulled her arm from his hold and dragged her heels. His gaze intent on her, he stood with his hands folded across his chest, his feet apart. She would have preferred it if he'd yelled at her.

His silence, however, eroded the edge of her anger, her resentment, and the need to explain was a pressing compulsion in her head. *He provoked the most unusual responses in her.* "I can't go with you. Believe me, it's better if you wait here for Kim rather than drag *me* to Paris."

The frost of his anger didn't thaw even a little. "Follow me," he said, and walked away.

Staring at his retreating back, she stood rooted to the spot, feeling like a dog being summoned by its master. Yet did she have a choice?

She drew the line at running after him like a supplicant.

She followed him with unhurried steps and found herself on the marble-tiled terrace. Beautiful solar lights placed at strategic points illuminated the vast grounds, and the rising sun was casting a golden glow over the grounds. Sprawling patches of green stretched as far as the eye could see, dotted with tall palm trees and occasional wildlife. Behind the mansion lay the ocean, and in front of them a picturesque lawn complete with a huge pool. For a minute the pristine beauty surrounding her captured her attention, and her elemental need to escape was buried under her awe.

It was stunning and peaceful. The mansion was a natural extension to the backdrop of the island. Except for the cluster of vans and tents parked outside the electronically controlled estate gates. She automatically counted them, finding fourteen vans in all. Something that very much looked like a long-range telescope was pointed at the terrace even now, and a babble of excitement surrounded it.

She instinctively ducked behind Alexander's solid body, disbelief shredding the peace she had felt mere minutes ago. "Are those…?" She couldn't even finish the sentence for the terror coating her throat.

"Reporters? Yes."

Fear wrapped its tentacles round and round her throat, cutting off her breath, dragging her into a ghastly flashback. Images she didn't want to see—of her tear-stricken face plastered across the newspapers. Sounds she didn't want to hear—of the rabble with microphones and cameras stuck in her face as her father hauled her across the courtyard of his house. And the uproarious glee of the bloodthirsty vultures when he had literally thrown her onto the street, proudly disowning her. They flooded her, sweeping her along on a tide of nightmare. Sweat dribbled down her spine and she moved closer to Alexander. She didn't care that she was clinging to him. She clutched the soft fabric of his sweater with her fingers, the warmth from his body penetrating the chill.

His hand snaked out around her, pulling her closer, until her chest flushed against his. The musky scent of his aftershave filled her nostrils. Even stricken with panic, her senses sighed.

"It will take them two minutes to figure out you're alone, five to corner you, even if you take my Range Rover, and ten minutes to realize you're the notorious Olivia Stanton. Even if you reach the airport unscathed without the help of my security force—*which is a big if*—this will cause a renewed interest in you, which means they'll dig up every piece of dirt they can on you, which I'm told is a lot."

Olivia risked another peek at the cluster and swallowed. No way was she going to step amid *them.* Not unless she had Alexander's army of high-tech security men in front of her *and* behind her. She licked her dry lips and set her mouth into a semblance of plea. "And the chances of you lending me your security guys so that I can reach the airport unscathed...?"

"Zero."

Bending his head, he kissed her temple, his warm mouth a searing brand against her sensitized skin. She struggled—purely a reflex. Only he pulled her closer. She opened her mouth to demand that he release her. But the words never formed. His hands crept into her hair and pulled her head back. His mouth hovered a few inches from hers. Her toes curled inside her sneakers. Every nerve ending inside her was crying for his touch even as another part of her screeched a warning. *This is wrong.*

Held still by his unrelenting grip, she stared at him. And felt a strange satisfaction flow inside. No, she wasn't going to kiss him. But that didn't mean she couldn't revel in the fact that he was just as susceptible to the treacherous desire between them. It was in the darkening of his crystal-blue eyes, in the thundering beat of his heart, in the sudden gentling of his fingers in her hair.

Yet Alexander did nothing without thought. Every move was a calculation in the big scheme of his perfect life. She was even more of an idiot if she thought he was as without control as she. She let her body go slack, willing movement into her trembling muscles. "You're pretending *for them*," she said, the truth a cold blanket over her heated skin.

His thumb traced a path over her cheek. "That should keep them happy for at least a day."

The fact that she was right was no comfort. "How did you know I was going to leave?"

"You're nothing if not predictable. And, just so we're clear, you pull that stunt again and I'll throw you to the wolves myself."

She averted her gaze from the hungry press, the horror of what she had been about to walk into sending a shiver down her spine. "For how long?"

His feet on the steps, he turned around. "Do you argue just for the heck of it? All I'm asking you to do is to spend a few days in the lap of luxury. Is that so hard?"

"If it means spending another minute with you—*yes*."

"You're at least unique in that," he threw at her arrogantly. "You have no choice until Kim's back. Then you could disappear to the North Pole for all I care."

His arrogant dismissal, the personal hit, let loose a fury in her. She hated the media, too, not hated, she *feared* them. Because they never let the world forget, never let *her* move on from her horrible mistake. Everything she had done since then, every choice of hers had already been forecast to doom, because her template was already preset to fail. And the moron that she was, she always delivered right into their hands. But it didn't mean she was going to stop trying, didn't mean she was going to rearrange her life to avoid them. "You're letting them control your actions, control your life."

His jaw clenched. "Don't push it, Olivia."

His dark warning only incensed her more. "This is about your pride, your image, isn't it? You can't be seen as the man who married the wrong woman, the less-than-perfect twin. God forbid that the world find out that you're prone to mistakes just like the rest of us normal mortals."

A smile, sharper than cut glass, curved his mouth as he pulled her toward him, two hundred pounds of intensity scorching her. "I've spent every waking moment of my life as a child haunted by the press. At seven, when my parents left me behind at a movie screening, at seventeen, when I was part of a criminal investigation. My childhood was like one of those bizarre reality shows based on Hollywood where nothing is sacred, nothing is left alone. *Only it was my life that everybody was watching.* I've been dragged through courts, have been studied like I was an exhibit at a zoo, have had stories written about me since I could barely talk. Enough fodder to last the press a lifetime. I don't intend to give them any more."

His face set into unyielding granite, he stood looking down on her. His words sounded as though they were coming from a dark place that warred with the cool exterior he presented to the world. His blue gaze glittered with pain. It robbed her of speech, questions she wanted to ask submerged beneath the overwhelming need to comfort him. "I walked away from that, made a different life for myself. But you know what? The shadow of it is never far behind. Do you know what that feels like? To have your every decision, every action studied, *dissected* under a microscope for even the smallest of mistakes, to know that the whole world, including your own damn parents, is waiting for you to fall."

She laughed, her bitterness spilling over into that sound. "Obviously, you don't know everything about me."

"I do. But you bring it on yourself with your reckless, indiscriminate behavior."

She flinched, each word a sharp twist in her side.

A hint of softness entered his eyes, and he moved closer to her. As though he regretted his remark. Yet whatever she had imagined, it was gone in a fleeting second. *A mirage.*

What was she doing? She was seeing things she wanted to see in him, letting her mind pull her down into an alternate reality. For some reason, she wanted to find a chink in him, something that would level the field between them. She was instantly at a disadvantage with anyone she met, her past a sword hanging over her head. And she didn't care, or at least she had painstakingly trained herself to not care. But with Alexander, she realized with a sinking sensation, all bets were off.

"Why do we have to go anywhere?" she said, hating the note of anxiety in her voice. She grabbed his wrists, ready to beg. She didn't know which haunted her more. The prospect of going back to Paris, or the looming pretense that she was his wife. Only a few hours in his company and she already felt as if she was coming apart at the seams, her armor already cracking. At least, here in his vast mansion, she needn't see the man unless absolutely necessary. "Why can't we just stay here until she's back and then you two can jet off to wherever you want?"

It was the hint of pleading in Olivia's words that hauled Alexander out of his own private hell. Until now, she had been all fire and lightning, like a Caribbean thunderstorm. Yet now, with her lush mouth pinched, she seemed anything but.

Reluctant concern sliced through him. No one wanted to re-visit their scene of crime. He understood that better than anyone. But he didn't have a choice, either. For more than ten years, he had kept himself out of the trash rags, taken care of his sister, and forged a different life. He didn't intend to let anyone wreck his life or his sister's, not the press, not his mother. "Because I have obligations, Olivia, people who can't wait to see me in Paris with my loving wife in tow.

"If word leaks out that you stood next to me instead of Kim at the ceremony, we'll become exclusive features on every damn channel, on every social media site. Not only will they hound me, but they will make your sister's life and yours, a living hell. So, if I have to endure your company until I can do damage control, I'll do it. And seeing the countless number of times your sister has saved your delectable ass, I would think you can bear my company a few more days, for her."

CHAPTER FOUR

NOTHING WAS WORKING.

Olivia blew at the stubborn lock of hair that kept falling into her eyes, and pulled her hair into a high ponytail with a vicious tug. She drew another picture on her notepad, her pencil flying on the paper and began to think of words for the pitch. The launch of Lifestyle Inc.'s sportswear geared toward everyday life was going to be one of the biggest launches of next fall. If she could bag the advertising contract for their agency, her career would finally be on the right track.

Her initial pitch to use social media for the ad campaign was what had resulted in their agency being shortlisted. Yet all the ideas that had been floating around her head seemed very insubstantial when she put them to paper. With a grunt, she tore off the pages she had so far and scrunched them up in her hands.

She knew in her bones that it was this place, this city they were in. The minute they had stepped off Alexander's private jet, it felt as though the iron lid she kept over her memories had been pried open by the warm summer breeze. She had just stood there, looking around her, transported back in time, the scents and sounds around her assaulting her. She had taken a breath of relief, when upon arriving at his penthouse, he had excused himself.

She had grabbed her notepad and sketches and retreated to the spare bedroom. She had been hiding since they'd arrived last night and all morning, venturing only into the kitchen for sustenance.

But there was no escape inside her own mind. Jacques's face kept pushing itself into her thoughts as though she had kissed him, begged him to not leave her yesterday instead of six years ago. Sweat beaded on her brow, her stomach a twisting void.

She had done everything in her power to keep him, to make Jacques love her, yet he had left her, trampled her heart into so many pieces. The same question she hadn't been able to answer that night or ever since haunted her waking thoughts now. She slapped her hands on her cheeks and shook her head, groaning, as though she could hold the devastating thought at bay.

But all her defenses crumbled like cardboard paper as it wound its way into her head.

Whatever she did, however much she tried, there were some things she couldn't change about herself. She couldn't...

No. She couldn't do this to herself. She cursed and swiped the tears pooling in her eyes. She had cried enough tears to last her a lifetime.

Scrolling through her BlackBerry, she read the text she had received from Kim early morning for the hundredth time. *I'm okay. Can't make it back yet. Am so sorry.*

The short message didn't tell Liv anything. The fleeting hope that she could get out of here soon died with it. She threw her bedroom door open and walked into the living room, refusing to indulge in miserable speculations that she already knew the answer to.

Alexander nodded at her from the couch, a sheaf of papers in his hand. He had been perversely silent all through the flight yesterday and even after they'd landed. Almost as if he knew how close to the surface her emotions were teetering. One wrong word from him and she would have clocked him. But of course, he hadn't given her that satisfaction. Instead, he had been a perfect gentleman all day.

She meant to ignore him but her gaze inevitably drifted down his body as he rose from the couch. Tight black jeans hugged his powerful thighs and *dear God,* the man had a taut behind she could ogle for hours. His gray V-necked tee stretched across the muscular contours of his chest, the short sleeves revealing strong forearms.

Heat crept up her neck as he neared her in a quick movement, the awareness of her perusal shining in his eyes. Her skin felt too tight on her body. He tilted his head sideways and studied her. "Are you approachable now?"

She shrugged and turned, glad that he hadn't mentioned her checking him out. The shards of grief that had dulled her mind into numbness mere seconds ago dissolved away.

Forbidden lust—1, gut wrenching grief—0.

Turning away from the captivating sight of him, she walked around the hall. Cream marble floors gleamed under her feet enhanced by white walls. Simple, sleek, red furniture dotted around the living room punctured the austerity of the pristine white. Understated luxury yet tasteful at the same time with a hint of warmth that had been missing in the island mansion.

The living room led into a vast balcony, offering breathtaking views of the Seine and the Eiffel Tower. A luxury private jet and a penthouse in the heart of Paris with such beautiful views, she couldn't help be impressed despite her dark mood. She traced the concrete railing with her fingers, feeling uncharacteristically peeved.

Alexander King might have turned his back on his A-list Hollywood star parents when he was only seventeen, but the fact that he was filthy rich in his own right incensed her further. Why couldn't he have been an abject failure like her?

And nothing she had seen so far indicated that he flaunted his wealth, unlike her father. No gold-edged trimmings in sight, no false imperiousness around his staff. On the contrary, his staff seemed too happy to follow his every command. He didn't need constant validation of his success. For all she knew, the man had been born with the arrogant confidence he wore like a second skin.

She turned back to the living room. A surprising sense of comfort settled in her stomach. Andy Warhol's turquoise Marilyn Monroe graced one wall. She passed by the Hollywood Diva with a grin on her face. The scandalous actress's painting in Alexander's penthouse looked as out of place as she had felt in the wedding gown.

"What are you grinning about?"

His voice behind her scrambled her senses. "I imagined it to be different." Spying the leap of awareness in his gaze, she hastened to clarify. "This place has such a relaxed feel to it."

"Meaning I'm uptight?"

She grinned again, unwilling to take the bait. "Meaning, is it yours?"

He glanced around the living room, as though looking at it anew. Something akin to affection danced in his gaze. "Emily decorated this place. She fancies herself an interior designer, so I gave her free rein last summer."

The sister Alexander guarded so fiercely? He had sued his own parents for custody of his six-year-old sister the moment he had turned twenty and had launched his own small business. The courts had granted him custody. The ruthlessness of the story made Olivia shiver all over despite the sunlight streaming through the windows. "Your sister?"

He nodded.

"I didn't see her at the wedding."

It was his turn to shrug. "She's busy."

He was famous for the utmost security with which he guarded his younger sister. Nothing about her was known to the public, which of course, made them even more rabid for information on her. "Too busy to attend her brother's wedding?"

Alexander shot her a warning glance, as Olivia raised her brows, her wide mouth an O. Emily would have enjoyed his wedding but he couldn't take any chances with her safety now. "Considering the farce that went down, it's better she wasn't there."

The censure in her words grated at him. And the fact that it *did* annoyed him even more.

It didn't help that he was already on edge. Nothing was going as he'd planned. Carlos, his head of security, had no updates for him regarding Kim, and his contact in Paris had confirmed his suspicions. Isabella had been living incognito in Paris for more than three months and it had nothing to do with her work. The fact that his mother was here where Emily went to school was not a coincidence. At least, Emily was away on a trip to the Swiss Alps with her school. And he had to depend on the one woman on the planet who was like a ticking bomb.

Olivia spent every waking minute feeling every emotion that passed through her. Every small joy had to be celebrated, like the fifteen minutes she had spent gushing over his flight attendant's wedding pictures. He'd expected her to rant and rage over him all through the flight for dragging her to Paris.

Instead, she had been unusually silent, her grief a dark cloud hanging over her. Any woman would have wanted to avoid the place where she'd had an affair with a married man, a man twenty years older than her, the place where her disgrace had made her notorious. He understood that. Yet it wasn't regret or even distaste for what had happened that she had felt. *Not Olivia.* Instead, he had felt her pain, her ache as though she had lost something precious in Paris.

She had reminded him of what he'd been before he'd learned to ruthlessly stamp out any feeling. It had taken everything in him to let her be. Feeding his dangerous curiosity about Olivia was not a smart move.

He frowned as she banged another kitchen cabinet door closed. He put the papers he had been signing on the coffee table and turned toward her. For a woman who was willowy and all bones, she was always looking for something to eat.

She stood on her toes, stretching her hands above her head, trying to reach the cabinet overhead. His breath hitched in his throat as her cotton tee tugged upward, baring her toned midriff, silky smooth flesh glowing in the light. His jeans felt uncomfortably tight.

With a muttered curse, he joined her in the kitchen and plucked the coffee filters from the cabinet. "Have you heard from Kim?" he said, more to distract himself from her scent.

Her shoulders stiffened, her hand faltering as she scooped coffee into the coffeemaker. Would she lie? He waited as she turned it on and her shoulders rose and fell.

She turned around and surprised him with a nod. "A text saying that she's okay."

He pulled out a couple of mugs and leaned against the counter. She almost collided with him in her hurry to get away, until he steadied her. Her T-shirt defined the curve of her high breasts and slim waist, and her legs went on forever in denim shorts that barely covered her behind. Her wild hair was pulled into a ponytail. She was all bones and angles, and looked like a teenager instead of twenty-five. She was a far cry from the women he found attractive—

successful, confident, exuding a sophistication that had always appealed to him.

Olivia was the opposite, not his type at all, yet something inside him reacted to her every move. And anything that didn't fall into a pattern, that defied rational explanation puzzled his analytical mind.

"Well, it seems like we're making progress," he said, grinning as she retreated to the other side. "You didn't lie to me just now and you didn't try to run away once in the last," he checked his watch, "fifteen hours."

One corner of her mouth tugged up in mockery of a smile. She poured the coffee into two mugs and handed him one. He followed her into the living room, eying her like a hungry wolf did a tasty morsel of meat. She took a sip of her coffee and plunked down into the leather couch. Her gaze swept around her, a smile curving her mouth. "I think Emily did a fabulous job. Too good to be a passing fancy."

"Unlike your new career?"

Olivia smiled, refusing to explain herself. It was what everyone thought about her, including Kim. While her loyalty and love for her never wavered, Olivia knew her single-minded, successful twin struggled to understand Olivia's impulsive choices. But all that was going to change soon. Excitement bubbled through her as she thought of her upcoming pitch. Finally, she had a real shot at succeeding, at forging a career. As soon as she worked on her pitch. "Not everyone finds success easily."

He settled into the couch opposite hers, his long legs stretching out to her side. "At least, you're a woman of multiple talents. Spoilt heiress, temperamental model, reality TV star and now what, advertising guru?"

The direct barb hit her hard, chipping away the veneer of politeness she tried to hang on to. Nothing he had quoted just now was untrue, yet the methodical listing of her failures shook her from within. But just because she had failed in the past didn't mean she would fail in the future. Love and men, she had given up, but her career—no.

"Exactly what is it that you find so objectionable about me? Because, from where I see it, I'm here, pretending to be your wife, when I never want to lay eyes on you again."

He laughed and set his cup down. The harsh sound of his laughter pressed against the bubble of tension closing in on them. "You did speak the words, Olivia."

She bolted from the couch. "They mean nothing to me."

"No, of course they don't," he said, leaving her no space to escape. "Tell me something. If I'm to believe you, you took Kim's place in a matter of minutes, vowed to be my wife without blinking an eye. I can't help but wonder how it's affecting your colorful love life."

She raised her brows and faked a smile. "Now you're concerned about me?"

"Let's say I want to be sure I don't have to defend myself against jealous lovers."

If only he knew the sad truth. No one had ever been jealous or protective of her, as twisted as that sounded. "I don't have a boyfriend, if that's what you're asking. Not—"

"Since that two-bit actor broke up with you on that reality TV show?"

No, not since then. Being dumped on national television had been the final nail on her relationship coffin. Of course, she had gone along, pretended to be okay with it because she had her pride. But after that, she had thought with her mind, not with her heart, looked up *self-preservation* in the dictionary. She took a sip of the coffee and swallowed down that ache along with it. "I'm worried about Kim. This isn't like her."

He shrugged, sending her good intentions flying. She stepped toward him, blocking him. "The woman you were supposed to marry is gone. And yet, as far as I can see, it's a mere inconvenience to you. Do you love my sister?"

A smile curved his mouth, cold and beautiful with no warmth to it. "Would you be happier if I was miserable, if I threw myself into endless parties and gave up all my responsibilities?" The knowledge of her past glinted in his gaze, underlined by something else. "Would you like me better if I behaved like you instead? Act on every impulse that runs through my head, run riot through everyone's life all in the name of love? I want no part of an emotion that strips a man or woman of rational thinking, that drives them to their lowest. So, by your definition, no, I don't love your sister. What I feel for her, what she feels for me, is much more rational."

Olivia stood rooted to the spot, her breath trapped somewhere in the base of her throat. *The lowest.* Yes, she had been there, and she had ended up there because she had fallen in love. But it was never going to be enough. She couldn't make someone love her. Whether it was her past, her failures or the total package she presented, no man was ever going to love her, not the love-you-no-matter-what kind. And for the most part, she had accepted the hard truth.

Except for times like now, when the truth smiled at her and gutted her, leaving her shaken to the core.

Alex cursed as Olivia turned away, a distinct shakiness to her movements, her face devoid of any color. Damn it, she had flinched as though he had raised his hand. *Where was his head?*

But no other woman aggravated him so much as her. She didn't have a filter between her brain and her mouth. She constantly argued with him, sometimes he was sure just to prove that she could. Why else would he have spelled out how distasteful he found her irreverence in gritty detail?

He tugged her around, his hand at her elbow.

The air around them cackled as she turned, her lower lip caught between her teeth. For a minute, he wondered if she was going to cry, if he had pushed her too far. He cupped her jaw and tilted it up.

She grunted, pulled herself away from his hold sending him backward where the couch hit the back of his knees. Suddenly, they were both falling into the leather couch, her slender body on top of his, their legs a tangle.

Her breasts crushed against his chest, her hands locked between them. The juncture of her thighs rubbed against his crotch giving him an instant hard-on. He shook with the need to pull her closer, to bury his mouth in the crook of her neck, to kiss her pinched mouth. Instead, he pushed her a little with his hands on her shoulders, anything to stop the soft press of her breasts against him. Every muscle in his body shuddered with the pressure to keep still. "You done?" he muttered through gritted teeth.

Pink seeped up her neck, drawing his attention to the pulse at her neck, frantic and pulsing. She moved off him, took a few steps back, her breathing harsh and shallow. "You provoke the worst in me."

He frowned, his libido still not under control. "Believe me, it's completely mutual."

She laughed, the sound strained with something he couldn't put his finger on. There was such a sense of defiance, a-devil-may-care attitude about her that it was hard to think anything could touch her. Yet his words had clearly hit a raw nerve. He dismissed the glimmer of concern that sliced through him.

"If you despise me so much, I can just leave."

He shook his head. He was letting her get under his skin. And it had to *stop* now. "There's an event I have to attend this evening and I need my wife there."

"And they say you're a genius businessman. A tip to

clue you in," she drawled, a bold gleam in her eyes. "Hurling constant insults in my face is definitely not the way to my heart."

He pulled the check he had signed earlier from his back pocket and extended it to her. "The last thing I want is your heart, Olivia, but merely your—" their gazes collided instantly, his hungrily running over her body, her face curiously devoid of color "—cooperation," he finished, wondering what he had said now.

She took the check from him, leveling her gaze somewhere at his chest. "What's this?"

"Let's call it a non-disclosure agreement that I would like you to enter. That you won't reveal to anyone while you're with me that you're the famous Olivia Stanton."

"You're paying me—" her voice shook as she advanced on him again, the hurt in her eyes replaced by outrage now "—to keep my mouth shut, to pretend to be Kim?"

"Or we could call it that."

"Why?"

"Because I haven't found anything else that's dear to you."

"To blackmail me?"

He ran a hand through his hair. "No, to get your cooperation. Any other woman would have agreed to it, if nothing else, for her sister's happiness. With you, I don't know."

"You think money will ensure my cooperation?"

"Yes. Even with all your business ventures, it seems you don't have two nickels to rub together. Kim bought your plane ticket to the wedding."

She advanced toward him again and right on cue, his senses came alive. Irritation flickered through him. She was the most tactile woman he knew with no sense of personal space. He flicked a hand through his hair and frowned.

But of course, she didn't heed his warning. She marched right up to him, effectively filling his vision with her.

She waved the check in his face, and he dragged his gaze to her face. Really, he was acting like a teenager. "Whatever else I'm, I'm not stupid, Alexander."

"No, you're not."

"So care to tell me why the big payoff?"

"I have already."

"Fine," she said, shrugging her shoulders. If he believed for a minute that he had her compliance, he was wrong. "But I don't want your money."

He snorted, anything to dislodge her wild rose scent from his nostrils. "And here I assumed you at least weren't stupid. Your outrage isn't going to pay the six months' rent you owe on that hole you call home."

"How do you—" Her words sputtered to a stop, her ponytail flying around as she shook her head. Olivia Stanton trying to rein in her temper. It was a rare sight, he was sure. "No, I don't even want to know." She scanned the check in her hand again, a glimmer of something in her eyes. "You know what? You're right. If I have to be here, suffering through your horrible, arrogant, *judgmental* company, I should get paid for it."

He grinned as she raised her gaze to his. "I'm always right. It's something you'll get used to."

"For whatever reason, you need me." A smile split her mouth, lighting up her eyes. His temperature spiked several degrees as she captured his hands in hers. "But I need something more than the money you threw at me if you want my cooperation."

He raised a brow. Her hands were still tucked in his, and it made him a little slow to answer. "It's not open for negotiation."

She went on as though he hadn't spoken. "I want your

word that you'll help me with the pitch for the advertising contract for LifeStyle Inc.'s new sportswear line."

Surprise made him slow to react. LifeStyle Inc. was one of his own companies. He lifted her and deposited her out of his way. "No."

She waylaid him again, her gaze earnest. "Before you jump to conclusions and call me a few names again, let me finish. I'm not asking you to do anything underhanded. Our agency has already been shortlisted. All I want is your help in understanding the ins and outs of how such a huge advertising campaign works. I've...never worked on something of that scale."

"Fine, you have my word. Not that it's going to make any difference. That sportswear line is the talk of the fashion industry right now. Whoever wins that contract must be extremely talented and hardworking." He leveled a look at her. Her eyes shone with excitement that he didn't want to crush. But she was only setting up herself for disappointment. Really, he was doing her a favor. "You've no chance of winning it."

Her chin went up a notch, the animation gone from her face. "I didn't ask for your opinion on that."

He grabbed his jacket and shrugged it on, fighting the insane urge to take back his words. *Why, when he had spoken only the truth?* "I'll return in a couple of hours. In the meantime, there will be a personal shopper here. Buy what you need for your stay."

"Why?"

"Because you're not going out with me dressed like that."

Her chin tilted up, her gaze blazing with a challenge. "Like what?"

With her luscious body outlined in the tight T-shirt and short shorts for every man's pleasure. The words danced around on his lips. But of course, he couldn't say that. A

simple conversation with her took more energy than por-
ing over a crumbling business's finances. "Like a street
urchin who hasn't had a proper meal in six months." He
ducked as she threw a velvet cushion at him and laughed.
"Which is probably true, *right?*"

"You're going to regret bringing me here," she said, her
gaze glinting with determination.

"Buy whatever you want, do as much damage as you
can. But don't forget that you're supposed to be Kim. No
fistfights, no arguments, no getting drunk and most of all,
no flirting with every man present. Even if he offers you
the whole world."

A shadow fell across her face. She swallowed, drawing his gaze to the slender column of her throat. "There's
no chance of me forgetting that. If not for Kim, I wouldn't
spend a single minute in your company."

Alexander shrugged into the Armani suitjacket and ad-
justed his collar. The breathtaking views of Seine and
Paris, twinkling in its glory, couldn't hold his attention.

His meeting had taken much longer than he had expected which meant he'd arrived with only a few moments to spare. His gaze sought the closed bedroom door
so much that he was beginning to memorize the pattern
of the wood. As much as he hated the recklessness that
embodied her every action, he had to admit he found Olivia exhilarating.

As if on cue, the door opened. His hands stilled on his
collar.

Her gold tinted brown hair, usually a mass of unruly
curls, was combed into submission and pulled back into a
knot at her nape. The severity of the hairstyle pulled every
sharp angle of her face into focus, adding to her sensual
allure. A red cocktail dress hugged her bodice, highlighting her generous breasts, dipping provocatively to her tiny

waist, before flaring out, ending a couple of inches above her knees. Gold colored sandals with their straps winding around her toned ankles completed the outfit.

If he looked at her with an objective eye, there was nothing provocative, even remotely scandalous about her dress, or makeup. Only he knew what lay under the elegant facade.

Yet he had never seen a sexier woman before.

Desire pounded through his veins, feral in its intensity. He rocked back on his heels, welcoming the fiercely alive feeling for a few seconds, enjoying her raw sex appeal. As he'd already told her, it was a natural reaction of his body. She would look sexy in a burlap sack.

Yet as he waited for the stab of lust to run its course, waiting for the moment he could control his body again, it never came.

The heaviness in his lower body increased tenfold as her hands smoothed over her tiny waist and her hips. Her shoulders pulled back, there was an inherent challenge in every line of her sensuous body.

She was bracing herself for an attack, not surprising after what he had said earlier. But then, she was always like that. Olivia always seemed prepared for battle, swords drawn as if she anticipated the world to throw the worst at her. And he had done exactly that.

He moved toward her, unable to turn his gaze away from the stubborn tilt to her chin, the gentle rise and dip of her breasts in silhouette as she turned, daring him to criticize.

He pulled her hand into his and crushed the sparks of awareness that shot through him at the contact. He slipped the diamond ring and the plain band he had found earlier on the kitchen counter onto her finger. Her hand shook in his grasp. He held it fast between them when she tried to pull it back, a surge of anger rising through him. Irrational, he knew, for whatever her faults, she wasn't responsible for the escalating intensity of his desire for her.

"Until Kim comes back, you're going to keep the ring on."

He met her challenging gaze and smiled, finding pleasure in the torture that was self-denial. Was that what she was?

A temptation, a challenge to test what part of him was his out-of-control parents and what part his own man.

CHAPTER FIVE

OLIVIA LEANED BACK into her seat and closed her eyes to shut out the seductive intimacy the luxurious interior of the limousine pressed upon them. Alexander didn't help matters, watching her with hooded eyes seated across from her. Really, the man had the longest lashes she'd ever seen. Which meant she could never really make out what he was thinking. The black suit fitted perfectly against the breadth of his shoulders, and with his hair slicked back, he looked like he belonged on *Mad Men*.

Their attraction shimmered around them spinning that web again. Even as they tried, they couldn't keep their eyes off each other, a dark heat surrounding them.

She turned with a sigh and caught her reflection in the tinted glass. She had spent all afternoon in the very capable hands of the personal shopper and a stylist, being plucked, groomed and polished to an inch of her skin. If they had wondered how Alexander King's very accomplished wife had nails bitten to the skin, they didn't let on. And she had thoroughly enjoyed being pampered. Being broke meant she hardly had money to buy nail polish much less a manicure.

Only now, looking at how polished and sophisticated she looked, how much like Kim, she felt the afternoon's bliss sliding off her as easily as the expensive silk of her designer dress. She was the exact image of her sister, the woman he wanted to spend the rest of his life with. Of course, Alexander was attracted to her. The thought spread through her like a vein of ice, stealing every drop of warmth from her skin. She shivered and pulled the cashmere wrap tighter around her shoulders.

God, how could she have overlooked the little fact? She had been brazen, finding perverse satisfaction in the fact that she threatened his control. But he had reminded her, once again, she was supposed to be Kim.

She ran a hand over her forehead, too restless to sit still, a perverse anger rising through her. Just looking at him got her heart racing, her concentration fragmented to bits. Of all the men on the planet, why did it have to be him who could threaten her good intentions? How was she going to be able to even face them when they were back together?

Her troubled thoughts stumbled as the limo came to a smooth stop. She tried to get a glimpse of their destination but a man in a black suit opened the door and tucked his head in. A swift exchange followed between Alexander and him and then the man closed the door behind him. A dark velvet box in his hand, Alexander settled next to her and the limo gained speed again.

She leaned back into her seat and crossed her legs as the solid length of his thigh lodged against hers, sending her pulse skyrocketing again. Distaste coated her tongue with a bitter taste as she realized what the box in his hand was. "I'm wearing my sister's ring. I'm with *her man,* pretending to be her. Isn't it enough?" Her throat caught on the words, her heart a squeeze of pain. She pushed the words out, more for her sake than his. It was a bitter reality but it was the only thing that could root her sanity. "Because no amount of window dressing is going to make me like her, transform what's inside. Believe me, I've tried." Tucking her hands in her lap, she threw him an irritated look hating the tremor in her voice. "And I hate diamonds."

He tugged her icy hands into his and held her gaze. It drilled into her, making mincemeat of her fragile defenses. But he didn't say a word. "I had a feeling about the diamonds," he said, his gaze still raking her, and clicked open the velvet case.

A huge ruby pendant nestled on a thin, almost-not-there gold chain.

She leaned back into the plush leather seat, panic swirling through her. "You ordered that between when we left and now? It must cost a…fortune."

He frowned. "It's a trinket, Olivia, something to wear with that dress."

Of course, it didn't mean anything. She turned around meekly. She took a deep breath, fighting for composure as he put the chain on her. The graze of his knuckles sent ripples of sensation over her skin. But there was no place for the warm, gooey feeling swirling inside her. The fact that he called a pendant that probably would pay for a penthouse in New York, a trinket, said it all. It was nothing but another step in ensuring her cooperation.

"Thank you," she whispered.

She ran a finger over the pendant, nestled in the valley of her breasts and his gaze followed it. She folded her hands in her lap and looked away from him. The quiet surrounding them scraped against her nerves. She needed chatter, something, anything to dispel the cocoon of desire spinning around them. "Did you ever want to be an actor?"

At his continued silence, she sighed. "So let me get this straight. You can pass judgment on every aspect of my life, but I can't even ask an innocent question about yours."

He raised an eyebrow. "Is it an innocent question?"

"Of course it is. Seeing that you're the son of Oscar-winning parents, and are particularly easy on the eyes, one does wonder."

"Am I?"

"Are you what?"

"Easy on the eyes?"

She shrugged. "You're the sexiest man I've ever laid eyes on, even when you're shooting daggers at me for one of my multitude of sins."

Heat uncurled in his gaze, the dark pupils shimmering against the blue. "The drama of my parents' life was enough to keep me away from anything connected to them."

"Do you ever see them?" She was skating dangerously close to the edge. His penchant for privacy was as widely known as his business acumen. But she couldn't stop herself. It was either engage her mind or her senses.

A warning glittered in those mesmerizing blue depths. "No."

The finality of that answer, the utter lack of emotion in it sent a shiver through her. No second chances, no looking back for Alexander King. Granted, in this case, his mother had shot his father, leading to one of the biggest scandals in Hollywood. "The press always makes more of it than it is."

"There's never smoke without fire, Olivia."

She tried to ignore the censure in his gaze, fought the urge to explain her past. "No. But sometimes, there's foolish naïveté instead of actual offense." Like her assumption all those years ago that once she was out of her father's control, her life would be a bed of roses, that she would forge herself a successful career, find a man who loved her. Like her sister's assumption that Alexander King was the perfect man. He was, if you lived in a world where no one ever made mistakes. The thought curled up around her chest, making it hard to breathe.

"Not in the case of my parents," he said without compunction. A shadow fell over his features, as if he wasn't in the present. "They were incapable of thinking beyond their needs, their desires or their passion, as my mother was fond of saying, as if it was just another great part she was playing. As a result, Emily and I spent months in and out of court, social services and the rest of our days haunted by the press. Is your curiosity satisfied now?"

Having pushed him into answering, Olivia didn't know what to say. At least, his sister would have been too young to understand much. But he had taken the brunt of it. It explained his obsessive need for privacy, to protect his sister, to control every aspect of his life and how it was perceived even. "I would have preferred it if my mother had shot my father instead of leaving."

A lick of fury came alive in his gaze and she wished she hadn't made the remark. "Why did she?"

She ran a hand over her throat. "Did you never ask Kim?"

He shrugged. "I know that it pains her to mention your mother. So I left it at that."

Bitterness rose like bile through her, choking her. *She abandoned us, Liv.* Kim's words rang in her ears. Yes, their mother had found an escape from their father, leaving them at his mercy. With their mother gone, he had turned his corrosive attention to them. But the one thing Olivia remembered despite her father's best efforts was the cloud of misery that had always surrounded their mother. "How perfect you are for each other, looking down your noses at weaker people, sweeping it all under the rug so that none of it touches you. Did Kim say our whole family was perfect, like her?"

He raised a brow, his gaze raking her. Her nails dug into her palms. "She could hardly claim that with you as her twin."

For once, his caustic comment hurtled her out of the past, from under the crushing weight of memories. She wondered if that's what he had intended. *A hint of kindness beneath the ruthlessness?* There she was again, imagining things that weren't true. "No, she couldn't." She tried to push away the memories to a corner. "That wasn't fair to Kim." Her twin loved her no matter what. "But it's the one thing Kim and I'll never agree upon. She never forgave my mother for finding escape, for leaving us with our father."

Alexander stared at Olivia. Because he understood Kim's anger. Even more surprising, because for all that he knew about Kim and her twin, he was learning that Olivia had suffered the most at the hands of her father. And she was the one with more sympathy for her mother. "And you have?"

She shrugged, her fingers laced tight in her lap. For once, the casual gesture, her well-worn defiance couldn't hide the pain glittering in her gaze. And it reached out and stirred a part of him he kept locked tight. "There's nothing to forgive."

"Nothing to forgive?" He couldn't keep the anger out of his words. "What kind of mother leaves her daughters at the mercy of a man she hadn't been able to cope with herself? Especially one like Jeremiah, who's a bully even in the boardroom."

"What if she had no choice?" she threw back at him. "It couldn't have been easy to cope with my father and us. I know, because she had never been in the best of health. Even before she left, I was a handful, failing classes, mixing with the wrong crowd, and every time I failed, he blamed her, called her a useless mother."

He pulled her white-knuckled fist into his hand, surprised yet again, by the jolt of sensation that ran up his arm. But he didn't drop it as every instinct in him warned him to. It scraped him raw, her belief that she was somehow responsible for what her mother had done. It was an abyss he was very familiar with, having climbed out of it through sheer will. "You cannot hold yourself responsible for her leaving, Olivia. Just because you weren't a model child doesn't excuse her." He should know, because he had done everything he could to be the perfect son and still it hadn't been enough.

She pulled her hands back, anger flashing in her eyes, dark and blistering. "Not everyone is strong and perfect like my sister and you."

He frowned, the fact she thought him perfect not sitting right with him. He was far from it. The fact that all he could think of at that moment was to lean forward and kiss her trembling mouth, sink his hair into her silky hair and muss it up as it had been before was proof enough.

No, he was just like any other man, one slippery slope away from temptation, from becoming that needy, hurting boy he had once been. Just thinking about the past filled him with shame. How many blows had it taken before he'd learned to not interfere between his parents, how many days of crushed hopes that he could somehow make it all better? How much self-discipline to get rid of the nauseous guilt even when he had finally walked out?

"No one who's known you could call you weak, Olivia."

Shock flickered in her gaze, her hands slow and shaky as she pulled the wrap closer around her. "You obviously didn't see me fleeing my father with my tail between my legs at the reception."

The bitterness in her words surprised him, even more so that it was directed at herself. She was a mass of contradictions, one minute—a fighter who didn't take any punches, the next—a vulnerable woman too aware of her own weaknesses. "Actually, it's what tipped me off that it was you and not Kim. And I understand why you did it. I've been a witness to Jeremiah's temper more than once.

Not every battle is worth fighting and it doesn't make you a coward." As he'd learned the hard way.

Her gaze flew to his and lingered. A smile curved her lush mouth, mischief dancing in her eyes. "Are you thanking me for not causing a scene at the reception?"

He laughed at the way she turned the tables on him. "Since you were the cause of it in the first place, no."

Olivia couldn't shift her gaze away from him. His mouth bracketed into deep grooves, his blue eyes crinkled with laughter, he was gorgeous, divine. His smile reached out like a wave, something deep inside her roaring in response. Looking away from him, she thought back to the afternoon when she had finally given into temptation and looked him up on Google. But she hadn't found anything *of a personal nature,* which was what she had been looking for really.

What she had found about him was enough to give her a complex, though. A successful businessman who specialized in investing in small businesses in dire need of capital, influential board member on a wide variety of charities, and even the women he had dated in the past— all successful businesswomen in their own right, had only good things to say about him. Alexander King, apparently, was the perfect man by all accounts. She thought she might be a little sick.

In contrast to her life, which was a comedic mixture of wrong decisions and desperate measures to compensate for those wretched decisions, his was a faultless canvas where nothing ever went wrong. Because there was no room for emotions, feelings or the mess they caused. Her gaze flicked to him and shied away, a chill sweeping up and down her arms.

Fortunately, the limo came to a stop again. With her hand in his, she stepped out, her gaze rising upward to take in the lavish building in front of them. She shouldn't have been surprised that the Ritz was their destination. Still, she just stood there, taking in the glamorous setting until Alexander nudged her with his hand at her back.

The moment they stepped inside, it was like entering a different world. Even her father, who looked down his nose at everything, would have been impressed by the deference shown to Alexander by the staff. She had very little time to appreciate the vaulted ceilings, the architecture around her before they were shown into what was a private banquet hall. She glanced around her luxurious surroundings, trying very hard to not gape openmouthed. Light glinted off the gold paneling on the walls, playing shadows with the sparkling fountain. Crystal chandeliers hung from the ceiling, the silverware twinkling in the shards of its light.

That feeling of not being good enough when she had been at one of her father's lavish parties returned with full force. She swept her hand over her hip, the exquisite silk of her dress restoring her nerves a bit.

"Stop twitching, Olivia," Alexander whispered into her ear, and she shivered. "You look absolutely stunning."

How did he read her mind so easily? Her heart flipped, and she forced herself to draw a breath, to not read too much into it. "So the point of us being here is that someone from the press will see us and come to the conclusion that everything is hunky-dory in your world?" she said flippantly.

His gaze scanned the private ballroom. "The point of us being here is that I have an important business meeting to conduct."

She looked around the impeccably dressed guests, couples smiling at each other, women checking out each other's designer duds. She made a mental note to thank him later for her own. Even the best dress in her suitcase would have made her stand out like a sore thumb in this crowd. "This doesn't look like a business meeting to me."

He nodded at someone on the other side of the hall

and pulled her in that direction. She stiffened as his hard body pressed into her, her skin singeing where he laid his palm on the bare skin at her back. "Not every business meeting is conducted in a boardroom. Some men prefer to cloak it under the guise of a pleasant evening. It gives them a chance to size me up. This particular one being of old school, places high value on propriety."

She stared at the middle-aged couple he was smiling at. "And you need to impress him?" she said, curious despite herself.

"Don't look so gleeful about it." His blue gaze twinkled. In that moment, he was the suave, astute businessman, the one that had been lauded on more than one business magazine. "Actually, it's he who needs my capital." She smiled, the pulse of his excitement a tangible thing. "Integrating his business into King Enterprises and bringing it forward into the twenty-first century is the challenge I'm looking forward to."

Of course. She nodded and smiled as they joined them.

Henry McIntyre looked her up and down shrewdly as Alexander introduced her. "I've been following your business's progress for a while now, Mrs. King," he said, his gaze razor sharp. "You're a rising star, and now that you have the sharpest businessman around on your side—" he tilted his gray head toward Alexander "—I'm sure you'll leave us all behind in a cloud of dust."

Olivia mumbled her thanks and settled down. Her hand trembled around the champagne flute as the older man went on in the vein of how perfectly matched they were in every way. She was no stranger to the fact that Kim was successful, as driven as Alexander. Yet Olivia had never felt the hollowness she felt inside. And it had more to do with the man sitting next to her than any career success Kim had achieved. Feeling like a fake of the worst kind, she leaned back against her seat and tuned out the conversation around her.

She was on her third glass of champagne when an excited, almost incoherent babble swept through the banquet hall, like a quiet drone of buzzing bees. Alexander and she turned at the same time. He stiffened in his chair, tension radiating from every inch of him, his skin a stark mask over the sharp angles of his face.

Olivia would have recognized the pair anywhere, even if they weren't Hollywood stars. Nicholas King and Isabella Fiori. The first thing that stuck her was how much he looked like them. He truly had the best of both the worlds. The second thing was that neither of them was as shocked to see him as he was to see them.

Alexander pushed his chair back and stood up, leveling a furious gaze at Henry, who fell back against the gilded chair.

"I owe her a favor, Alexander. Just hear her out."

Alexander shook his head, his features set in stone. "You've just lost the chance to save your business."

His words were coated with a dark fury that drew a line down Olivia's spine.

"Alexander?" she whispered as he tugged her up.

He didn't respond. Just stared at the approaching couple, his eyes cold and hard. Squashing the questions pounding inside her head, Olivia returned the pressure on his fingers, hoping to get through to him, to break the bubble of emotion that held him immobile in its hold. But he didn't move, not even a flicker of eyelid.

The silence in the hall prickled along her skin. She swallowed as she looked around. Every gaze in the banquet hall was focused on them with greedy curiosity stamped across their faces, an indecent hunger as though they couldn't wait to see a crack in the man they all envied, to see him bleeding.

She bit her lip. He loathed losing control, yet he seemed oblivious to anything around him. Her mind made up, she stood in front of him and cupped his jaw. He still didn't look at her. Pulling some air into her lungs seemed hard work, her heart revving up faster and harder at what she was going to do. She swept her hands into his hair and pulled his head down. The tangy scent of him pervaded her as she arched closer and pressed her lips to his.

She only meant to snag his attention for a minute, to distract him from whatever it was that choked him in its grip.

Instead, his hands crept up her back, circled her nape, pulled her into his hard body with a force that knocked the breath out of her. Her breasts crushed against the wall of his chest, the juncture of her thighs cradled by his, every line of muscle in his body pressed against her shaking ones. Her shocked gasp misted into nothing as he made a rough sound in his throat, and crushed her mouth with his.

Warm and soft, his lips flushed against her lower lip. He tasted like whiskey, like pure, torturous heaven. He pressed his advantage, his tongue invading her mouth, erotic as it dueled with her own, and the intoxicating taste of him exploded inside her mouth. Heat, unlike anything she'd ever known, slithered low and furious in her belly, curling into pinpricks of pleasure all over.

She had wondered about this moment since the minute she had laid eyes on him. Yet reality was nothing like she had imagined. There was no seduction, nothing civilized, nothing *controlled* about what he did to her. He prodded and plundered her mouth, drew her tongue into his mouth, his actions almost savage, as if he needed her taste to sustain himself. A moan escaped her as he nipped her lower lip, his harsh breathing puncturing the sexual cloud fogging her senses. She tilted her head away from him to pull some air, and his mouth trailed over her jaw toward her neck. It was so tempting to stay like that, to take whatever he gave, to let herself go.

But she couldn't ignore the little voice that said he really didn't want to kiss *her*. She couldn't forget she was a stand-in and for her sister, of all people. The passing mention of Kim was enough to electrocute her drugged senses back into reality.

She cupped his jaw, the pads of her thumbs tracing the grooves around his mouth. "Alexander? Get a grip, or I swear I—"

He cupped her face and tilted it up in a rough movement, his gaze blazing. As if he didn't want to stop. After only a few seconds that felt like another eternity, he nodded and pulled her to his side. Just as his parents reached them. She could feel their gazes upon them. She ran a hand over her trembling lips as she turned around.

"Hello, Alexander." Isabella drawled his name, her accent thick. Liv searched her voice for a trace of affection. The very lack of emotion sent alarm bells ringing through Olivia. "It is good to see you."

Alexander didn't move or bend his head even though it was clear that his mother wanted to kiss his cheek. Nicholas King didn't utter a word, either. Only stood at his wife's side, his blue eyes, hard and flinty.

"Isabella," Alexander said. "I would call it a pleasure but we both know I don't have your talent for acting. So let me get straight to the point. What the hell are you doing here?"

The silence that followed sounded like a deafening drumbeat to Liv's ears.

Isabella smiled, not betraying her reaction even by the flicker of an eyelid. But then, the woman hadn't won an Oscar for nothing. "We are married again."

Alexander's fingers dug into Liv's flesh as his grip tightened on her shoulders. If he had been angry before,

Liv didn't even have a name for the blistering emotion pouring out of him now. "And you thought I would want to celebrate the good news with you?"

He turned Olivia with him, half dragging her toward the exit.

"No," his mother said behind them. "I want to see Emily. And I won't let you stop me anymore."

It was only because she was flushed so close to him, in tune to his every breath, to every nuance in his face, that Liv felt the imperceptible shudder that ran through him. And it sent a pang of ache shooting through her.

But he didn't turn around. Only halted long enough to utter, "No."

And just like that, they walked out, Olivia still reeling with shock.

CHAPTER SIX

OLIVIA THREW HER metallic clutch onto the coffee table and followed Alexander into his bedroom, teetering on the heels. The ride back in the limousine had been filled with nerve-racking silence, punctured only by Alexander's numerous calls on his cell phone. He hadn't given her a chance to interject a word.

The sound of a shower running in the bathroom halted her footsteps at the entrance to his bedroom. He didn't want her there. She knew that as surely as the tingle she still felt in her lips. But she didn't care. Something had happened and she had no idea what. And she wasn't going to leave the room until she had some answers.

She undid the winding straps of her sandals. The lush carpet felt heavenly against her bare feet. Moving to the French windows, she pulled the dark curtains away. The king-size bed, complete with black silk sheets, drew her gaze, robbing her mind of everything else. She swallowed hard, wanting to run her hands over the silk, the scent of him rapidly drugging her senses. And that's how Alexander found her.

Staring at his bed like a sex-crazed twit.

A black towel tied low on his hips, he ran a hand through his hair. "Leave, Olivia."

Her gaze drank him in, her breath stuck in her throat.

He wasn't overtly muscular, yet there was definition to every muscle in his chest. His hair, still wet, clung to his scalp. Rivulets of water slithered down his chest, tugging her gaze to his washboard stomach and disappeared into the towel. She scrunched her brows as if she could telekinesis the towel to drop.

She knew she heard him, because she felt the responding signal from her own brain. *Move. Run.* Yet it seemed her muscles were incapable of following up. Her skin tingled all over. She licked her lips, rubbed her fingers absently over her nape. Dampness pooled at her sex and yet the man hadn't even touched her. The sound of his towel hitting the floor, denim sliding over his skin, every cell in her was attuned to each sound he made.

And then he was right in front of her, his bronzed chest rippling with muscles, unzipped black jeans hanging over his hips. Her stomach dipped and dived. "Olivia?"

Her gaze hitched on the strong column of his throat, the corded muscles in his neck. "Hmm?"

"Stop staring and Get. The. Hell. Out." Her gaze flew to his. His gaze devoured her, the naked hunger in it stripping all rational thought from her. "Or God help me, I won't be responsible for my actions."

She shook her head, ignoring the free-falling in her stomach. "I'm not leaving until you tell me what tonight was about." He took a deep breath and his impressive chest fell and rose with it. "When was the last time you saw them, Alexander?"

"It's really none of your business."

She steeled herself against his anger, against the onslaught of sexual tension spiraling around them.

"We crossed that line when you dragged me here." She turned the diamond ring on her finger, its cold, unfamiliar touch never far from her thoughts, the thought that it would be only this particular one she would ever wear in her life a painful reminder. "Think of it this way, the sooner you answer my questions, the sooner you will be rid of me."

"Nine years ago, in court."

Shock rendered her speechless for a few seconds. That explained why he had frozen like that. "But you knew they were in Paris?"

"I knew she was. I've heard rumors that she means to sue me for custody of Emily."

A heaviness gathered low in her stomach. It was almost as if a curtain fell away from her eyes. His insistence on her accompanying him to Paris, the check, his shock at seeing Isabella with his father, everything neatly slotted into place like pieces of a puzzle. She walked circles around him, her mind grappling to understand.

With a possible custody battle coming, of course he couldn't risk a scandal. "Is this why you dragged me to Paris?"

His silence was answer enough.

"She wouldn't really engage you in a custody battle, could she? I mean, they could just be rumors." Even as she said that she couldn't shake off the utter lack of emotion she had spied in Isabella's eyes.

He laughed, a harsh sound that sent ripples of fear skating over her skin. He roamed the huge room, which seemed to be swallowed up by his restless energy. He seemed surrounded by a fortress of emotion, like a bellowing volcano struggling to contain itself, nothing like the man she had known so far. *Or was this the true him?* "My mother? She's capable of anything. Except being a mother."

He reached her before she could blink, invading her personal space. The heat from his body sent tingles up and down her skin, his scent sending her heart into overdrive. "Is your curiosity satisfied now? Are you happy that after all, I'm a flawed man, no better than you?"

Something had changed in him at the party. The suave,

heartless businessman was gone. He was seething, his emotions tangible in his aggressive stance, in the way every muscle in him bunched tight, ready to strike. And she was in the direct line of fire. Still, Olivia couldn't force herself to move. He was in pain. Her heart contracted with ache. She didn't know why or how she knew that, but she did.

"I'm not." She forced her throat to work past the fear. "The idiot that I'm, I want to be here, with you." She licked her lips, and he moved another step closer.

His gaze narrowed on her lips. "Why?"

She shrugged, unwilling to look into the whys of it. "You just don't seem like yourself. You need to let it out, Alexander. Tell me what you're thinking. Do something, *anything*. Throw that glass at the wall. I swear you'll feel much better."

His thumb flicked her lower lip, and his gaze drilled into hers. He was thinking about their kiss. Suddenly, she wasn't sure if she really wanted to know what he was thinking, not in this strange mood. "You want to know what I want to do, what would make me feel infinitely better?"

Her knees turned into jelly. Before she could even frame a response, he pulled her hard into his body, his hand curled around her nape. A ragged sound escaped her as his arousal rubbed against her belly, his other hand shaping her hip. The flimsy silk of her dress was no barrier between his hard body and hers. Pangs of desire shot through to the apex of her thighs, only his hand on her keeping her upright. "Do you have an idea now?"

Every nerve ending within her screamed with tightening need as his hands moved up her bare arms. "I want to kiss you again. I want to rip that dress off you, throw you onto my bed and bury myself inside you. Until I can't move or think anymore, until every cell in me is so numb that I don't feel anymore."

A tremor traveled from her nape to her toes, her skin was on fire with need.

"Unless you're up for that, get out."

She pushed him back with her hand, feeling a sudden chill. Like a concrete wall, he didn't even budge an inch. "You don't want me, you want Kim." She wasn't sure who needed the reminder more, *him or her*.

"There isn't a single moment that I confuse you for Kim anymore."

Her gaze flew to his. There was no disdain or the scorn she had become so used to seeing. Only naked desire. And it messed with what little sense she had left.

Alexander stared at Olivia, at the shadow that fell over her expressive face as she uttered Kim's name. But it didn't have the intended effect. Nothing could puncture the potency of his desire for her now, of the fury, the grief raging through his blood, seeking an outlet.

And what an outlet it would be.

She stood out like a siren in her red dress against the backdrop of his black sheets. The exposed skin at the neckline shimmered brighter than the silk of her dress, her silky hair fighting the confines of its style, every rise and dip of her curves enticing him into temptation.

Before tonight, he had only wondered at his attraction to her, at the way his senses felt so wired into whatever she did, that it was nothing more than a reaction of his body to hers. *He had been wrong.* There was nothing simple about the way he reacted to her.

"It might never go as far as a custody battle, right? I mean your mother said they just want to see Emily."

Her smile, her obvious delight that his problem was solved shifted something inside him. He had trained himself to not need anything from anyone, and her concern in the face of his harsh words seeped into his blood. Like a whisper of a gentle wave that could easily become a sweep of a violent storm that he couldn't contain. Like a drop of poison that could pollute the whole stream.

Because seeing Isabella and Nicholas together had already made a dent in him. It was as though the self-control, the discipline he had acquired over the past twelve years had disintegrated into dust at his feet. His mind had flipped back to his childhood, shuffling through a reel of pictures, drowning him in memories he didn't want, crumbling the defenses he had built.

His parents' constant fights, Nick's vicious anger, Isabella's elaborate power plays to keep his father's attention, Alexander's own innate need to protect her, his failure to do so, his pathetic attempts to win her love, to be better, smarter, to excel…as if it might buy her love, as if it might divert her attentions for one second from his father to him.

God, the list went on and on….

Sweat trickled down between his shoulder blades.

And as a man who had always acknowledged his own limitations before he destroyed them, Alexander admitted the truth to himself.

He wanted Olivia with every cell in his body, with every breath he pulled into his lungs. It would be sex, it would be escape, but it would also be so much more. Because he'd had a taste of what she could give.

With one kiss, she had dragged him back from the edge. From the fury, from the dark, shameful spiral of his own thoughts. And he had kissed her, reveled in taking everything she gave like a sinking man who had been thrown a lifeline.

She could have just stood there, watched him lose the tenuous hold he had had on himself and let it all go to hell. Yet she had stood by him, pulled him back from the edge in a way only she could have thought of. Her loyalty despite everything he had said to her clashed against his belief that she was selfish to the core.

Even now, her concern, her stubborn stance in seeing him through this, they washed over him, prying open things he had locked away a long time ago, things he never wanted to feel again.

No.

He stepped back from her, the hollow sensation in his gut blaring like an alarm. He didn't want her, he didn't need her concern, on any level.

It was only by emptying his life of any need that he'd survived. He could go even so far as to say he was a slow learner, couldn't he? Because it had taken the worst to happen before he had stopped clinging to that hope that one day his mother would leave his father as she had promised so many times, to shed the fear that he would one day lose her, to overcome the guilt that he wasn't enough to protect her and himself.

Control, over his fear, over his guilt, over the debilitating need to gain his mother's love, that's what had helped him survive.

"You will let them see her, won't you?"

He dragged his gaze back to her, steeling himself against the worry in hers. "Stay out of it, Olivia."

Of course, she didn't. She moved closer to him, her fingers gripping his forearms. He felt her tremble, saw her fight to draw her next breath, her dismay at how easily the need between them flared into life, unraveled them. And still, she didn't run away. "You're hurt, Alexander." Looking at the warmth brimming in her chocolate gaze, he braced himself. It was more deadly to him than anything else he'd encountered. "She didn't even ask after you. She didn't—"

"Stop. Just because I admitted to wanting to screw you—" with each word he fought for control until the emotion sifted out of him "—doesn't mean I need or even welcome your concern."

"But—"

"*Enough.* Don't you think you're taking this pretense a little too far?" He watched like the heartless bastard he was as her face lost its color. "You're, after all, a stand-in. You're not obligated to hold up the whole *through better or worse*. I appreciate what you did for me back there but it doesn't have to continue here."

She drew back in the slightest of movements, an imperceptible jerk of that stubborn chin. Her hands shaking, her slender shoulders held stiff, she moved to the door. "Of course not. I mistook you for a different man, someone who could still *feel*. But thanks for the reminder that you're incapable of that emotion."

Alexander ran a hand over his eyes, feeling as though a crack had inched around his heart. But he couldn't let it spread. If anything, seeing his parents was a timely reminder of what he could become if he let himself feel.

CHAPTER SEVEN

OLIVIA BIT INTO the chocolate filled-croissant and stifled a moan as the butter and chocolate melted in her mouth. The pavement café adjacent to Alexander's building was a little slice of heaven. She had taken to spending most of her time here rather than spend one unnecessary minute with Alexander cooped up in the penthouse.

She had stayed up a few nights, and worked on her pitch, the ideas flowing as she strove to capture them on paper. Now all she had to do was create the presentation and her pitch would be ready. She closed her eyes and leaned back, a smile curving her mouth. The warm, late-afternoon sun caressed her skin. The faint hum of traffic and chitchat enveloped her without jarring her thoughts, which of course, revolved around Alexander.

He had mostly left her to her own devices the past week, during the day at least. But, in the evening, it was another party, or a charity event or in the case of yesterday night, an intimate dinner with friends.

Ever since the night they had encountered his parents, there was a difference in him. Of course, he was back in perfect control, whereas all she had to do was close her eyes to taste him on her lips.

He was polite with her, didn't throw insults in her face anymore.

He had even made her coffee in the middle of the night when she had been rubbing her eyes determined to finish her work. And when she had promptly fallen asleep with her chin on the table, after drinking the coffee, he'd put away her work neatly, picked her up and tucked her into bed. All through the week, he had let her pick his astute brain, had explained to her all the elements that went into making a marketing campaign a success, without mocking her.

By all accounts, he'd been exceptionally nice to her. She should be glad about it.

But she wasn't. Not that she would welcome the Alexander who'd been so brutally honest with her, outlined her every failing. But he'd been well, *honest,* with her. She had known exactly where she stood with him. Now that she had seen a glimpse of the real man beneath, the one who felt pain and grief, the one who had openly acknowledged the attraction between them, she couldn't forget the savage need that had glittered in his gaze before he had pushed her away ruthlessly.

Even knowing that he had been in pain, knowing that he despised having revealed himself to her like that, she still liked that man.

She leaned back in the seat and clutched her stomach. When had she become such a masochist? Hadn't she already learned her lesson more than once? What else would she have dared if he hadn't pushed her away?

Guilt coiled through her belly, raking its nails over her insides. Of all the men in the world, why did she have to be so drawn to her sister's fiancé?

"You're hiding from me."

She jerked straight and tucked her hands in her lap guiltily.

Standing right above her, Alexander cast a dark shadow over her, stealing the sun's warmth. She shivered as the sheer presence of him pressed on her. Dark and brooding, his expression was in direct contrast to his white shirt.

She swallowed as his gaze swept over her. It hesitated for an infinitesimal moment over her mouth, his pupils expanding against the blue, sending a lick of heat through her. She could feel the tightening of her cheeks, the flush creeping over her neck. She clutched her legs together under the table, glad that she was sitting down.

She straightened up in her chair, and folded her hands. There was a boldness to his gaze, a decisive set to the line of his mouth that scared her.

"I'm not hiding," she said, the words sounding breathless, not at all like she'd intended. Her heart raced as he pulled out the chair next to her and settled on it. "However, I might beg them to let me live in their kitchen forever."

He smiled, even though it didn't reach his gaze. Her arm moved against his as she reached for the last bite of her croissant, sending a tingle up hers. Just as she brought it to her mouth, he deflected her hand toward him, his grip at her elbow gentle and firm. His mouth closed over the tips of her fingers as he tugged the croissant into his mouth.

She reeled back, sensation exploding over every inch of her. She watched as he chewed and swallowed, the movement of his Adam's apple, the dark glitter in his eyes holding her captivated. He didn't moan or gush over it, only nodded in understanding.

The silence shrilled around them. She fidgeted in her seat, wanting to move away from him. She opened her mouth and just as quickly shut it as he leaned back. Something was wrong. She didn't want to ask, she didn't want to care, he had clearly drawn the line between them. But she hated this awkward tension between them. "Alexander, what's wrong?"

"Why would you think anything's wrong?"

"Because you have that look about you." He raised an

eyebrow, a challenge in his expression. She exhaled on a whoosh. She was beginning to understand him a little now, was beginning to pick up the little signals that meant his emotions were far closer to the surface than he would have her believe. "Like you would like nothing better than to inhale me whole."

He threw his head back and laughed.

She continued as though he hadn't interrupted. "Only then, you wouldn't like yourself for what you've done so you'll spit me out again, uncaring of how that makes me feel. I'm not a punching bag for you to hit whenever something angers you. I'm here because Kim asked me to, whether you believe me or not. And—" she swallowed as his gaze searched hers, his attention never wavering from her face "—for reasons beyond my understanding, I'm attracted to you. So stop yanking my chain. Whatever our differences, I thought you a better man than this."

He cupped her chin, pulled her closer and all air left her lungs. He angled his face and leaned in. It was the perfect position for him to press his lips to hers. She trembled as he watched her like a hungry hawk. Torture methods probably had nothing on what this man could do to her with just a glance.

"I'm not yanking your chain." His breath breezed over her lips, sending a ripple of longing through her. "I've been fighting the insane urge to kiss you, to strip you of every inch of clothing and take you, until neither of us can move an inch much less think about the right or wrong of what we've done. It's a madness in my blood." The pad of his thumb brushed her lip. "And before you say I'm pining for Kim again—" his gaze became distant and hard "—let me make it clear for the last time, that she never ever evoked anything as uncivilized in me as you do."

She pushed his hands away and slacked against the chair, her breathing shallow.

"There. Does that make you feel better?"

The tone of his words could slice through the cup in her hands. "No," she said loudly, her senses slowly coming out of the fog he seemed to spin effortlessly.

"Not even a little kick at the sexual thrall you have me under?"

Her heart kicked against her breast. *"No,"* she repeated louder, a surge of anger diluting the thrill his words did evoke. "I understand that what would be a minor matter of an inconvenient attraction to any other man is of utmost significance to you. Because your control over what you let yourself feel is what defines you, isn't it? And the fact that you can't lock it away, that you can't turn it off is driving you nuts. So, *no,* I can't rejoice in the fact that you despise me because you're failing in your own eyes."

"I don't despise you, Olivia." He tilted her chin in his hands, his touch infinitely gentle. It took everything within her to hold his gaze. "It would be easier if I did but I don't."

"No? Only yourself, then," she said, feeling battered. After that night, she knew how much it cost him to admit what he did just now, yet she felt nothing but hollow inside. How could she be so drawn to a man who was out of her reach on every level there was? "When a man is attracted to me, I want him to embrace the fact, not think it's beneath him. Whatever my past mistakes, I deserve that much." Her words sounded confident, defiant even, yet the fact that she had never met such a man nor probably ever would was a painful knot in her stomach.

She braced herself from some caustic remark about her past. Instead, he tucked her arm around his and leaned back into his seat.

They sat in silence like that for a while. A warm and fuzzy feeling uncurled in her stomach as she studied his profile. Even as she fought it, the truth crept in. Alexander, she realized with a slow, agonizing breath, could crumble her good intentions to protect her heart with one simple look or a heartfelt smile.

"Carlos informed me today that Kim never left the island," he said, gazing straight ahead. "She's still there."

Olivia pulled back with a jerk, guilt a constant, heavy shackle she couldn't shake. It was like a house arrest bracelet that screeched every time her heart ventured into forbidden territory.

Tight grooves bracketed his mouth. "I was a jerk when all you did was help."

She tried to remind herself of the anger, the frustration she had felt that night when he'd blamed her for everything. But she had to admit that anyone who knew Kim would have doubts believing that she had fled her own wedding. For a man who dealt in absolutes, who never was plagued by doubts, Kim's actions wouldn't make sense, especially because he had believed her to be above it all.

"That's all I get?" Her heart beat a stuttering tattoo against her rib cage. "If I remember right, I said I would settle for nothing but a grovel. And before you say you don't know how, let me tell you. You go down on your knees, spread your arms wide, kiss the ground at my feet and say 'Oh, great Olivia, please forgive me'."

He burst out laughing, the sound of it rippling over her. A couple of women stumbled to a stop by their table and slid long glances at him. But his gaze didn't turn from her.

"That's what I like about you, your unending optimism." His eyes sparked blue, the curve of his sensuous mouth lifted at the corners. He looked breathtaking, laughter etched into the stark lines of his face. "What can I do instead of *the grovel?*"

"Keep smiling like that."

His sinful mouth still curved, he shot an eyebrow up.

Breathe, Liv. "I mean, you rarely, if ever, laugh." She drew her brows together in mock seriousness. "It's always—make sure Emily's okay, make sure my billion dollar empire is fine, make sure Olivia is not up to trouble. I agree the brooding look is definitely sexy, but when you laugh, you just…" She sighed, and shut her mouth, the amusement inching into his gaze heating up her cheeks.

He leaned forward. "Maybe it's the present company that hasn't given me much reason to laugh? Between figuring out where Kim is and trying not to forget I have *some* sense of right and wrong, which believe me is very hazy right now, maybe brooding is all I have left."

Loaded silence hummed around them for a few seconds before they both burst out laughing.

"After dinner, we can—"

She shook her head. "No. I can't stand another business dinner."

What she couldn't bear was the sense of inadequacy that was becoming second skin again. She had spent the better part of her life wishing she was more like her twin, had barely managed to train herself to accept that she would never even come close.

And every second she spent with Alexander, a little of that acceptance crumbled.

When he opened his mouth, she forged on, refusing to let him interrupt. "Even couples honeymooning need a break from each other, don't they? Or if that ruins the image of perfect marriage you're supposed to have, you can tell them I'm tired from all the crazy monkey sex we've been having…"

Their gazes collided and held, her breath hitching in her throat. The blue of his pupils darkened. He leaned back into his chair, moving his neck this way and that. "Crazy monkey sex, huh? Is this your way of punishing me because I didn't believe you? Because it's working."

She stood up on shaky knees.

"I'll cancel tonight's dinner. There's a runway show that you might like."

Warmth exploded in her chest. The fact that he belonged to Kim should be more than enough to kill the attraction. Her sister loved him, *deserved* him, and even the unbidden rush of pleasure Liv felt at the prospect of spending the day with him was wrong. "You don't have to spend—"

"We're family. It's time we learned to get along."

She fell back to the cobbled ground with a *thump*. "You really know how to make a girl feel all special inside, don't you?" She glared at him. "If you're worried I'll make a spectacle of myself somewhere—"

"I'm not." He grabbed her wrist when she pushed her chair back, locking her in place. "I'm extending the olive branch. We're going to feature in each other's lives whether we like it or not." His thumb moved over her skin, sending flares of sensation rippling over her skin. "And I had no idea how hard all this was on you."

She *had,* but for all the wrong reasons. With each passing day, Jacques had moved further and further back in her mind, Alexander now occupying the front and center position. She locked her trembling hands in her lap.

Nice move, Liv. From frying pan into the fire.

Refusing to meet his gaze, she pushed her cup back on the table. "Pfft… This…*thing* between us? Being attracted to totally unsuitable men is kinda the running theme of my life, as you already know." She really deserved an award for her acting skills. "It's you who seems to be—"

"I mean—to pretend you were Kim."

She hated how easily he saw right through her, how easily he turned her inside out with a few kind words. "I love my sister. I've never begrudged her her success or anything else that she's achieved." That was mostly true, except for the man staring at her with an intensity that could crumble her already-weak will.

He nodded, his gaze searing through the false smile she forced to her mouth. She yanked her handbag over her shoulder and stood up, eager to escape.

Leaning his head against the chair, he closed his eyes. She greedily drank the sight of him without the piercing gaze assessing her. "The limo is at your disposal. Do what you want."

"I don't want…" He was right. He was going to be a permanent fixture in Kim's life which meant she had to learn to tolerate his presence without going all hormonal and moony over him. Or at least learn to act normal despite feeling hormonal and moony.

"Were you serious about us spending the day together?"

He shrugged in that I-don't-give-a-damn kind of way.

"You *really* are good for my ego."

"At least I'm not recoiling at the idea as you seem to be." He opened his eyes and leveled a curious look at her. "Would it help if I said I was *mildly* looking forward to it?"

"Okay, I can live with *mildly,*" she said, tongue-in-cheek. "But you have to give up the control-meter for once."

"The *what?*"

He looked so uncharacteristically slow that she laughed. "I'll decide what we're going to do and you have to go along."

"And what's that?"

"Oh, come on, Alexander. This is going to be fun." She clutched his hand and tugged him up, knowing exactly what he needed. She *was* getting better at breathing through the thump-thump of her heart as his large brown hand enclosed hers. "You know, doing something spontaneous and crazy, something you can't control to the last minute, *fun.*"

Alexander had never felt such unrelenting curiosity before as the limo took off through the streets of Paris and entered the A1. All through the drive, Olivia refused to reveal anything, literally bouncing in the seat.

He felt like a kid who had been granted a special treat, at least that's how he imagined he would have felt if he had been a carefree kid. When he moved to lower the tinted windows to get a clue as to their destination, she batted his hand away. "Don't make me blindfold you."

He listened with increasing amusement as she chatted on about the time she had spent in Paris before, about the changes in the city, the number of times she had gotten into trouble and not once did the shadow of her disastrous affair mar her lit-up gaze. He had no idea what had changed but he was extremely glad for it.

Grinning from ear to ear, he leaned back into the seat, his curiosity spiking exponentially with each passing minute. He already knew they weren't going anywhere formal. With her hair tied up in a high ponytail, dressed in denim shorts and a Hard Rock Café tee, Olivia looked unbelievably cute, not that he could tell her that. And she had made sure he had dressed down, too, in shorts and a polo T-shirt.

Today, more than any other day, since they had arrived, they looked exactly what they were pretending to be. A couple honeymooning in Paris with no pressures from the outside world, drastically different from what he would have been doing if Kim were here. Even the reminder of what Kim had done didn't dilute his excitement.

The limo came to a smooth stop. "You ready?"

He nodded, the eagerness with which he was looking forward to it quite novel in its intensity.

They stepped out of the limo, and a drone of excitement reached his ears. He tucked his hands into the pockets of his shorts, and looked around, a strange little pang clenching and unclenching his gut.

Happy voices and smiling faces washed over him, the buzzing din of it rippling along his skin in an unfamiliar way. Unfamiliar but not grating. He didn't know what he had expected. But it hadn't been this.

They were at an amusement park. It was a perfect summer day, and the park was filled with kids and adults making the best out of it.

His first instinct was to turn around and walk away.

He stood unmoving as Olivia waved away the chauffeur and sauntered toward the ticket booths. Almost as if she knew to let the place and the noise around them seep into him for a few minutes. His gaze followed her hungrily as if she was his lifeline. The only time he had been at a park, of any kind, had been on his seventh birthday when he had spent the few hours watching his parents fighting like alley cats and paparazzi parked outside the gates.

The slight dimming of Olivia's smile as she reached him with tickets in hand knocked the memory on its head. If nothing else, he would stay to not spoil the day for her.

Her gaze lingered on him as she waved the tickets. "What? Don't tell me your time is too precious for a roller coaster."

He fisted his hands in his pockets, striving to keep his tone normal despite the strange heaviness in his throat. "I've never been on one."

She widened her eyes and fluttered her lashes innocently, or as close to innocence as the minx could manage. "Oh, really? Then you're in for a treat."

He rolled his eyes and smiled, letting her tuck her arm through his. "I'm glad you've given up on being an actress. Because, frankly, you suck at it."

"I wouldn't be so sure." She nudged him forward and they fell into a comfortable stride. "And before you get ideas, the only reason we're here is because after almost a week of pretending to be supersmart *and* in love with you—I'm not sure which was harder by the way—I need to unwind."

He looked sideways at her. Her skin glowed in the sun, her eyes twinkled. "Why am I even remotely surprised that an adrenaline-pumping roller coaster is what would loosen you up?"

Her teeth dug into her lip, and she stepped to the side, giving him a once-over. His pulse pounded. "Actually, what would loosen me up is a good, hard bout of…"

He wrapped his hand around her wrist and tugged her closer, the mere scent of her skin incredibly arousing. "You think this is funny?"

"No, but what else do you expect me to do? It is either laugh at the whole thing or…" Her brown eyes darkened. "Well, you know what I mean."

She moved in front of him, her back to the crowd behind her. "All this deprivation and control, it might be good for the soul, but it does nothing for the body."

Within an hour, during which they stood in line for, of course, the scariest ride in the whole park, Alexander realized how wrong he was in thinking that Olivia would be in her element on the roller coaster.

Even as excitement rose in his gut as they settled into the car and it gathered momentum across the track, inching upward toward the high point where the track started looping in, he felt Olivia tremble next to him.

She was wedged tight against him as the car careened to one side, and even with everything else around them, his skin thrummed at her nearness.

He opened his mouth and breathed through the rising hum around them, his heart pounding in his chest. He felt the grin spread across his mouth, feeling a liberation he had never felt before.

He laughed, the sound barreling out of him, as they entered a downward loop, the wind blowing in his hair, adrenaline pummeling through him. And this time, he could see their reflection in the water below as the track threw them facedown.

Olivia's white-knuckled grip tightened on his hand, while her other hand tightened around his arm. He turned to tease her about squeezing too close to him, but the words froze on his lips.

Her skin bereft of color, her features frozen in stark terror, Olivia screamed at the top of her lungs as their car veered into another loop, throwing them upside down from a height from which people on the ground looked like colorful dots.

She screamed, the sound edged with terror.

As the third loop approached, she was shaking uncontrollably next to him, her hands clammy. His threw his arm around her shoulders and squeezed her closer to him, the strange sensation in his gut standing out even amid the thrill thrumming through his veins.

By the time they had reached the penthouse, Alexander didn't have words to describe the day. Even in thought. The quiet joy of the evening was, quite literally, something he had never experienced before.

Olivia had been right. It was the most fun he had had in...*forever*. And it wasn't just the insane roller coasters, either. It was her company, her pleasure in the smallest things that had done it. They had gone on three rides, gotten their picture taken in a booth and he had even won her a stuffed toy.

He couldn't remember a time, even when he'd been a kid, when he hadn't been mired by a sense of responsibility and until this moment, he hadn't realized how much of that he had carried into his adult life.

He had made millions through sheer hard work, had taken responsibility for his sister when he'd turned twenty and he had never learned to laugh, to live for the moment, to lose himself in the sheer pleasure of everyday things. He hadn't even known what he'd needed or what he'd been missing. But one thing he hadn't missed was the fear that Olivia had felt throughout each ride.

Her long legs folded under her, she leaned back into the couch and blew out a tired breath. He swallowed and pulled his gaze from her graceful neck. Her brown eyes twinkled as they met his. "So what's the verdict?"

"You want your pound of flesh, Shylock?"

"Yes."

"It was more fun than I've had in a while."

Her eyes bright, she smiled. She didn't need to give a hoot whether he had or not. But she did. And the warmth in her smile stole through him.

"Even better, we didn't argue," she said, her gaze slipping to his mouth for the fraction of a second.

Too tired to fight his own impulses, he watched her hungrily as she walked to the refrigerator and pulled out an ice cube.

Being attracted to her when he'd considered her a selfish, scandalous epitome of everything he despised had been easy. But she was slowly turning every arrogant assumption of his into dust.

Every nerve in him tightened painfully as she ran the ice cube over her cheeks and neck, wetting her t-shirt in the process. "Thanks for today. It was a lot of fun except when you refused to share your cotton candy with me."

He laughed out loud. "Well, you were already hyper and every time we were on one of the rides, you looked decidedly green. Now I know you're not as fearless as you behave. Did you go on those rides just so that you could cozy up to me?"

She threw the ice cube at him. "You really think you're irresistible, don't you?"

He fisted his hand over the ice cube, the idea of a cold

shower sounding better and better. "Not so funny now, is it?"

"Good night, Alexander."

Shooting up from the couch, he tugged her arm. "You were terrified for every single second of those three rides. I kept waiting for you to throw up, or to say enough."

She shrugged. "I know. Every time I go on one of them, I tell myself this is the time I won't be scared. But it never works that way."

"So you've done this before?"

"Yep."

"And yet you still go, knowing that you're going to be terrified?"

"I will never know the thrill unless I do, will I? And it's a roller coaster. It's not like it might kill me."

"That's how you do everything in life, don't you?" His question was loaded with accusation that instantly killed the curve of her mouth. But he couldn't stop himself. "You jump on it for the thrill and to hell with the price you might have to pay."

"You make me sound like an adrenaline junkie."

"More like emotion junkie."

"Well, of course, I jinxed it, didn't I? Truce over." She folded her hands, gearing up for a fight. "Stop messing around and just tell me what's bugging you."

He felt a familiar sensation pummel through his blood, something that had once almost destroyed him. He didn't want to feel the concern tightening his chest, especially for someone like Olivia.

Because Olivia didn't need anyone. That was her appeal, her wild defiance of every convention, her absolute acceptance of herself. Yet his analytical mind couldn't stop seeing the pattern of why or how she did things.

Until now he had attributed it all to recklessness, to

sheer lack of concern for everything in life but her selfish pursuits, yet he couldn't hold on to that belief now.

He caught her elbow and turned her toward him. The same pervasive thrill ran through him at her nearness.

God, he'd never been so tempted to kiss someone like he wanted to kiss her, never wanted to defy his own set of rules, everything he had built his life around. Until he met Olivia, his control, his will, had never really been tested.

"Not every thrill in life needs to be chased, not every emotion needs to be explored until it consumes you. And not everything you chase is as harmless as the roller coaster, is it?"

She tugged her hand away from him, her posture stiffening. "I don't know what—"

"Your affair, your careers, your choices in—"

She paled, her gaze stricken. "You think I had an affair with Jacques for the thrill of it?"

"No, I'm saying you've gotten into the habit of chasing the wrong things just so that you could find some validation, to find some…. It's okay to say enough, to cut your losses, and even better to take control and walk away."

"I know failure, Alexander. It's been my longest friend."

He shook his head. "Walking away from something that's not good for you doesn't equate failure. It takes just as much courage as to succeed. Believe me, I've been there."

Olivia stared at him. Just hearing the same words *failure* and *Alexander* in the same sentence was enough to silence her.

Tilting her chin up, he pressed a kiss on her cheek. "Good night, Olivia."

Olivia slid against the leather, her arms and legs boneless as he walked away from her.

She ran a hand over her cheek where he had kissed her, tried to breathe past the fluttering in her stomach. She had always attributed her failures—in anything she had done, to herself, to her own faults and weaknesses.

Alexander's words turned the assumption on its head. There had been no contempt in his words, no derision. They had rung with belief, even concern, as though it had mattered to him that she see things his way.

In that moment, she wanted to believe him.

The gentleness in his words seeped into every pore of her. She lay back against the leather and closed her eyes, replaying the evening again.

Because, without doubt, it had been the best day of her life.

CHAPTER EIGHT

THE NEXT MORNING, Olivia pressed the power button on her laptop for the second time and muttered a curse. She had a few minutes before a conference call with her boss, Nate, and of course, her years-old laptop was messing with her again.

As the blue screen took forever to load, she settled down on the couch just as Alexander slid toward the other end. Her laptop still hadn't powered on.

He slid a new, glossy laptop, a pink one like her own, but of course, the state-of-art expensive model into her lap. Her mouth wobbled as she struggled to string a coherent sentence together. "What's this?"

He didn't look up from his iPad. "I noticed that your laptop takes a while to reboot and thought you might like a replacement. It's all set up. All you need to do is transfer your files from your old one."

He extended his hand, palm up, and she stared blindly for a few seconds before she grabbed the flash drive from him.

Not trusting her vocal glands to work past the wedge in her throat, she mumbled something. Or tried to. It was a simple gesture, nothing that would have cost him time or energy. Yet it was more precious than the pendant, or the check he had given her or anything she had ever received in her life. For a minute, she ran her finger over the gleaming surface, fighting the tears prickling behind her eyes.

Clearing her throat, she plugged her headphones in and powered it on, quickly transferring her presentation when her old laptop finally booted up.

She made notes and answered Nate's questions as he brought her up-to-date. Excitement thrummed through her as he walked her through his notes on her presentation.

But she couldn't shake off the unease dripping into her when an awkward silence descended on the line. "I'm sorry, Olivia, but—"

Something was clearly wrong, especially because Nate was never one to mince words. Whether praise or criticism, she had always found him to be fair-minded.

The sound of her own breathing curled up dread inside her. "Nate…whatever it is, just tell me."

Alexander frowned, reading an email from his lawyer. Tightness knotted in his gut as he read on. Isabella had finally set things in motion, even though it was cloaked under a request for an initial hearing to review their visitation rights. He didn't believe for a second that it would stop there. The rumors weren't just rumors anymore.

Which meant he needed to strike first.

He needed to plan, he needed to call his lawyer and figure out the best way to handle this. Damn it, he needed his wife by his side.

But not even the pressing email could hold his attention when Olivia's call took on a strange note next to him. She kept repeating the same words, her face pale.

"I do understand, Nate…No, I get what you mean. It's just that I've…" She swallowed, her words ringing with misery. "Yes, okay."

Her eyes glittering with tears, she yanked the headphones out. She slid the laptop into the couch, shot to her feet like a coiled spring.

He reached her in a minute, the tears she scrubbed viciously from her face freezing him into inaction. He was so used to thinking of her as defiant and strong that he couldn't believe that they were tears, that she could be hurt. He gripped her wrists and pulled her closer. "Liv, what's wrong?"

She shrugged, her mouth a bitter slant. "I'm not going to be working on the pitch to LifeStyle Inc. anymore."

"Why? I've seen how hard you've been working on it, the merit of your ideas."

"I—"

He wanted to reassure her that she could trust him. Yet it could turn into a false promise in the blink of an eye. With any other person on the planet, he could give his word knowing that he would keep it. With Olivia, there was no telling what she would say and how he would react.

She rubbed her trembling hands over her eyes. "LifeStyle Inc. has a new marketing director."

"Yes, Vincent Gray. I appointed him three days ago. What's that…" His words faltered as things clicked into place.

She had slapped Vincent at his engagement party to Kim, broken a contract with him before. "Vincent knows better than to hold personal grudges in the work environment." When she didn't elaborate, he continued. "But no one can change the fact that it will make working with him a difficult situation for you." He softened his words, hating that he had to speak them. "Nothing justifies unprofessional conduct."

"No, it doesn't. That's why I have been re-assigned. So that I don't jeopardize the agency's chance to win the contract, even though it's my idea that got us shortlisted."

"What the hell does that mean?"

"Nate's afraid that if I head the pitch, Vincent, at best,

would make it hard for the campaign to go successfully, at worst, won't grant the contract to our agency."

He frowned. "Irrespective of the content or the suitability of your campaign?"

"Yes."

"You do have a lot to learn if you think that's how my companies do business. This is not a campaign to sell lemonade on a roadside stall, Olivia. What you're suggesting is not only highly unprofessional but unethical. If someone made such a statement publicly, it would be grounds to sue for defamation."

"It's not that simple, okay? You can spout all kind of rules from here but the reality is that…."

"What?"

She walked away from him, wound up in her own world.

"Don't do this," he said, pulling her back to him. He didn't know why he cared so much, only that he couldn't let it go. "With the reality show, you had to have a relationship with the lead guy. With the jewelry campaign, you up and quit, and instead of making contacts and building a reputation in advertising, you slapped Vincent at that party. Why did you quit that campaign if you're serious about a career in advertising?"

For the first time since he'd met her, she didn't meet his gaze. "Does it matter?"

"Yes."

"He…harassed me sexually."

Alexander froze, wondering if he heard her right. "I've known Vincent for ten years. We started working on our first business venture together. I've never even…" He ran a hand through his hair, things he'd always been confident of in his life shifting before him. "Are you sure you didn't misunderstand him, you didn't…"

Olivia laughed, a bitter sound that echoed around her. Tiny cracks inched around her heart. It was what she had expected him to say. And yet she couldn't believe how much it hurt. Just because they'd spent a few days under the same roof looking beneath the surface, coming to an uneasy truce didn't mean Alexander saw her any different from a car crash. If she'd expected any different, even on a subconscious level, then she was an even bigger idiot than she had thought.

"Am I sure if from the minute I started working at the jewelry firm, Vincent kept hitting on me? Yes. Am I sure if I heard him right when he said, *'Women like you can never say no'*? Yes. Am I sure if he criticized every tiny bit of work after I, somehow miraculously, managed no? Yes. At your engagement party he said the reason Nate had given me my job was because I was *putting out.* So, yes, I slapped him."

"I just can't believe Vincent would—"

She clenched her teeth, holding the dam of ache rearing to burst through inside. "Whereas I've had an affair with a married man, have no material success to give me even a little bit of credibility and have no talent to speak of. So of course, it's not a big leap that I would be lying."

Alexander closed his eyes and swore softly. Her words could have been plucked from his mind. He didn't want to think them yet his rational mind couldn't stop. And yet hearing her give voice to it, nauseated him. "I didn't say that."

She sidestepped him, and made her way to her bedroom. "You didn't have to."

He pulled her back toward him, perverse anger rising through him. "I'm not done —"

She twisted, struggling against his grip. "I'll punch the daylights out of you if you say one more thing."

His grip on her arms tightened, and he pulled her closer, until he could see himself reflected in her brown gaze.

"That kind of behavior is what landed you here, Liv. I'm trying to help—"

"No, you're not. You're being a rational, analytical jerk again and I won't take it."

She twisted in his hold again, and this time he forced her against the wall, their harsh breathing surrounding them. Adrenaline pumped through him, anger and arousal roped together inside him. "Stop it, Olivia.

"Why didn't you report him?"

"Do you believe me?"

He wanted to say yes, yet his mouth wouldn't form the word.

She slackened against the wall, and sighed, a depth of pain in it. "Either I would've gotten the creepy, twist-my-gut silence I'm getting from you or the much worse 'she asked for it'. I found neither idea particularly palatable. Because, after all, it's not possible that I don't want to sleep around with every man that looks at me, right?"

His gut tightened. It was exactly what he had assumed about her, what he had set out to prove that night on the beach in his anger. Was he no different from Vincent, then? "What're you going to do?"

"There is nothing to do."

"Is that it? You're ready to give up so easily?"

She glared at him. "Yesterday, you were telling me to accept—"

"Yes, to make better decisions, to walk away when you feel the need to shack up with the wrong guy again."

"How long have you been waiting to throw that in my face?"

Alexander could feel his head throbbing, his meager control on the situation slipping. He was doing this all wrong. Why did a simple conversation with her become such an exercise in control? "I didn't ask you to give up on something you've worked so hard for.

"How is anyone ever going to take you seriously if this is how you react to each hurdle? If you do win this contract, you whole agency's future will rest upon the campaign. And let's face it, however hard you work now, you can't wipe away your past. There are always going to be people who will hold it against you."

Every inch of color fled from her face.

"So maybe it is better for everyone involved if you walk away now. Your kind of quitter mentality isn't something I want associated with my company's campaign, even indirectly. And I bet that's what's bothering your boss. Not that you might not win the contract but that you will never successfully see it through."

"I hate you."

"Do that, Liv," he said, releasing his grip on her with great effort. The pain in her eyes unraveled something inside him, but he forced himself to utter the words. "Blame me all you want if it helps you cope with the fact that it's easier for you to walk away."

Alexander leaned back against his seat as Olivia regaled one of his oldest friends, Mike, who was also visiting Paris, with another one of her stories. It was their last dinner out before they left for New York the day after. He was waiting for a call from Carlos, he had a thousand things on his mind and he shouldn't have been able to enjoy even a minute of the evening.

Olivia had shot that theory to hell in a second.

The low lighting of the small pavement café on Champs-Élysées, another of Olivia's divine finds, threw shadows over her, giving him teasing glimpses of the curve of her mouth, a slender shoulder or, if she bent a certain way, her warm, gorgeous smile.

She had dressed simply in a denim skirt and a gold sequined top. The silky fabric moved sinuously over her torso, hiding and showcasing her lithe figure, driving him crazy. It hooked at her neck, leaving her glorious back bare. It was all he could think of since she had walked past him to the elevator.

He watched, arrested, as she laughed. Her face lit up, her shoulders shook with her mirth. "The next thing we know, our wing warden walks by and all the girls are blowing rings into the air."

He smiled. He could almost see that teenage version of her, all attitude and sass, the first one to jump feetfirst into one more escapade at the boarding school, the first one, from all the snippets she had shared, anyone in trouble went to.

Her gaze flicked to his instantly, cautious, as she backtracked and added that she had many more stories about her wild twin.

Mike winked at her, a grin curving his mouth. "Olivia sounds exactly like my sort of woman—sexy and fun."

Olivia pulled a bright pink Post-it from her clutch, scribbled her number and slid it toward Mike. A fierce pounding began behind Alex's right eye. "Why don't you give her a call in a few days? She would *love* to hear from you."

Alexander pursed his mouth, and wrapped his arm around Olivia's shoulders. And instantly felt her stiffen beneath his touch. Her hair was pulled back into a tight plait, and his fingers itched to tug it free and sink into it. He still couldn't stop sliding the pad of his thumb over her bare skin, though, perversely enjoying the right to touch her.

She was still angry with him over their discussion about Vincent. But there was nothing he could say to make her feel better. Except his absolute belief in what she said. But Vincent still hadn't gotten back to him. He knew, in a corner of his heart that didn't look at facts and figures, that she was telling the truth. Yet he couldn't bring himself to say the words, could barely admit to himself that...

Of all the damned things, when had he started thinking with his heart again?

Cursing himself for what was surely becoming more than a momentary madness, he pulled his hand back. *What was wrong with him?*

His iPhone buzzed. Seeing Carlos's face on the small screen, he excused himself and walked into the twinkling Paris night. He knew from Carlos's brief emails and Kim's continuing silence that it was not going to be good news.

Carlos didn't mince words. "Kim is married, Alex. I waited to inform you until I could verify the authenticity of what I discovered and I have. I have a copy of their original marriage certificate. And even though she had filed for divorce several times, the man she married never signed it. Their marriage is valid under law. From what I gathered, she...is staying with him."

Fisting his hands, Alexander let out a curse that resonated around him. Fury ran rampant through him as every word Kim had ever said to him flashed in his mind. The veneer of perfection, the unblemished reputation...he had bought it all.

He stood frozen, his anger swirling around him, pounding through his blood. The depth of her lies and deception blazed a tidal wave through his gut.

He had trusted her with everything, and she had done what?

Risked exposing them both to a huge scandal. She had even put Emily's custody at risk. Everything he had worked for could have been jeopardized.

For a moment, all he could think of was to punch the nearest wall, to give into his baser impulses for once. To let every control mechanism he had developed go to hell.

"Alexander?"

Olivia.

He uncurled his fingers and counted to ten, trying to

regain control over himself. Her scent, familiar yet arousing, fluttered through him as she neared him. Her fingers clamped over his wrist, she pulled him toward her while her anxious gaze searched his. "Is everything okay?"

Perverse laughter choked up his throat as he gazed into her beautiful eyes, the haze of anger and something else lifting from his eyes. It was a moment he would never forget in his life.

The woman he had thought perfection personified hadn't had the decency to tell him the truth that could have plunged him into the biggest scandal of his life—on the scale of his own parents' indignities and into committing bigamy whereas the woman he had mocked and insulted, whose very irreverence had grated on him, had stood by him, again and again, concern lighting up her gaze.

So much for his absolute arrogant belief in his judgment, for his carefully thought-out plans.

His gaze fell to Olivia, to the stubborn tilt of her mouth and his hands tightened around her waist. Pure, scorching emotion, something he didn't want to analyze, engulfed him. "You're not going out with him," he said stiffly, nodding in Mike's direction.

"Watch me," she threw back challengingly. "And anyway, who died and made you lord and master of me?"

It was like striking a spark to dry cinder. Without hesitation, without second thought, Alexander dipped his head and kissed her. He swallowed her protest, the taste of her lips, the warmth from her body, what he had once considered a trivial temptation that was beneath him, stole through him, rooting him once again back to his sanity.

Only when she opened his eyes did he see the shadows of hurt in her gaze. She wiped her mouth with the back of her hand, her mouth a bitter slant.

He stood frozen, watching her as she walked back to

their table. What the hell was he doing, kissing her like that? Especially now.

He needed to consult his lawyers with regards to Kim, he needed to sort out the mess his life had become. With the judge agreeing to an initial custody hearing, and now with Kim's announcement, he needed Olivia to continue the pretense as his wife more than ever.

Which meant, he needed to stop winding her up, he needed to…

And yet…look at the way he had kissed her just now. As though it was the most natural thing to do, as if it had been more important than his next breath. Every muscle in him tightened to a rigid mass as something shifted within him.

Had he trained himself so well that he was impervious to the whispers of his own heart? How had he assumed to continue with Kim and their marriage as though the firestorm that Olivia was hadn't blazed through his life? Had he really become that heartless?

Throwing her scarf into her suitcase, Olivia closed her suitcase with a satisfying thump. Sighing, she walked into the attached balcony.

Her gaze took in the beautiful star-studded night around her. The glittering lights, the light breeze, it was a beautiful Paris night. Yet she had never felt so wretched. Despite hating his unemotional attitude toward life, she had still given Alexander power over her. Why else would his disbelief about Vincent hurt so much, why would she feel as though a void was opening up inside her at the thought of leaving?

Tomorrow, they would be back in New York. The next time she saw him, he would be with Kim. Her chest hurt with every breath she took.

But it had to be this way. Alexander could so easily.… *No.* She wasn't going to indulge in self-pity.

She grabbed her BlackBerry and scrolled through it. *A missed call from Kim.*

She clicked Call, every nerve in her tuned so tight that she thought she might snap, come apart at the seams.

She forced herself to pull the crisp evening air into her lungs as Kim picked up on the other line. "Liv…I'm sorry you got stuck there. I—"

Olivia fought to keep her tone normal. "That's fine. Now, what's going on and when are you retuning?"

"God, he hasn't told you yet…"

Olivia swallowed. Her stomach lurched. A cold chill settled over her skin. "Tell me what?"

"It's over, Liv, between me and Alexander. He—"

Olivia stood shaking from head to toe, incapable of forming a response. "What? Why? I—"

"I left before the wedding because…" Kim's words broke on a catch. "I'm married, Liv, something I did years ago. And just after you arrived the morning of the wedding, my divorce papers came back unsigned."

Shock rendered Olivia incoherent for a few seconds. "What? Who is he? When did you… I mean, why have you never even talked about this?"

"I… It was the summer after you had left, Liv. I—"

"You mean after dad threw me out," Olivia couldn't help correcting. Of course, Kim could have walked out with her, except, doing something her father didn't approve of was fundamentally impossible for Kim. Even though she had done everything in her power to help Liv.

"I met him on a cruise and I…fell for him."

"Hard enough that you married him?" Her shock made her words hard. Olivia couldn't even continue as another thought stuck her. "If you're already married, why did you… Where does Alexander come into this? You said you didn't want to lose him. And yet knowing him, you put everything he considers important at risk."

When had she become the sensible Stanton twin? If she wasn't consumed by confusion and sadness on top of so much else that she couldn't even identify, Liv would have laughed out loud at the irony of the situation.

"It's just that after so many years, I wanted a new start." The wretchedness in her twin's words did nothing to alleviate Olivia's confusion. "And Alex was so perfect. He appreciated me, he never asked for more than I could give. I never intended going back on my promise to Alex, Liv. Except the past fortnight has been—"

Liv clutched the metal railing, her legs threatening to give out under her. "Wait. Are you staying with this man?"

"I just feel so much, Liv. I think he…"

A knot twisted up in Liv's gut. She was glad that Kim was okay. *She really was.* Except…even after everything, her twin had her perfect ending, another man who loved her. "Of course he does. You're the perfect woman. How could any man not fall in love with you?"

How could any man who had known that perfection want a flawed fake instead?

"But I couldn't bear it if you were mad at me."

"I'm not, I want you to be happy," Olivia said, trying to soften her tone. For the first time in her life, her sister had done something she wanted, not because their father had deemed it right. And yet, Liv couldn't drown out the rapid tattoo of her heart, couldn't help feeling as though she was the one paying the price, even for Kim's indecision. "I just wish you had told us earlier, Kim."

"I intended to return—"

"Even after a week?" Olivia said, clutching her phone tight. "Were you still figuring out who the better option was?"

"I'm not like you, Liv. I'm… I know what I have with Alex is not the real thing."

Her throat choking up, Olivia listened in silence as Kim

apologized again and hung up with promises to catch up in New York. Only one thought ran circles in her head.

Kim and Alexander were over.

Her knees were shaking, her hands clammy. She grabbed her handbag and jerked it over her shoulder. She needed to get out of here, needed to get a grip on herself before she...

She ran straight into Alexander. Every inch of her tightened, thrumming with awareness.

His gaze raked her, a frown on his forehead. "Olivia, are you okay?"

She turned toward him, her internal balance instantly toppled by his consuming gaze. The light blue dress shirt made his eyes light up. Dear God, he was gorgeous, he was sexy and he was *not* her twin's man. She swallowed and stepped back.

"I just spoke to Kim," she whispered, staring absently at her phone. "She said it's over..." She frowned, struggling to breathe. He looked as calm as ever, his gaze eating her up. "How long have you known?"

"Since yesterday."

The news had toppled her entire world. Alexander hadn't even betrayed himself by a flicker of an eyelid. "And yet you didn't say a single word. Are you so incapable of feeling anything?"

CHAPTER NINE

ALEXANDER POURED A shot of whiskey from the decanter and gulped it straight down. He had spent the whole day telling himself why giving into what he wanted was not a good idea.

At that moment, he had absolutely no idea why.

He turned around to face her and felt the muscles in his stomach tighten. She looked glorious. He wanted Olivia, the intensity of that want, of that desire was feral, robbing any good sense from him.

Her breasts fell and rose with her anger. Color slashed those angular cheekbones at his thorough appraisal. "I don't want to talk about Kim."

Her chin lifted. "I don't care what you—"

"I spoke to Vincent. I know you were—"

She blinked. "And you decided to believe me *after* speaking to him?"

"He denied it, said you were the one who came on to him. But I know he's lying." Paradoxically, Vincent's defensive denial, the very tone of his words had done it. In the end, he hadn't needed proof. So much for not trusting his heart. "I made a huge mistake. But there's nothing I can do about it, Liv. The terms of his employment contract require proof. It's your word against his."

Olivia stepped back, her mind reeling. With every word

he uttered, he was swallowing up the distance she wanted to keep. She could fight his arrogant accusations, even his low opinions of her, but when he was like this—a man who could admit to his mistakes, a man who wasn't perfect, she was utterly lost, defenseless.

Panic bubbled up through her. She felt as if she was split in half, one half greedily drinking in every word he said, every look he leveled at her, reveling in it while the other half whispered constant warnings to stop this, to run as far from him as possible. And the worst part was she had twenty five years of experience ignoring the second half.

She searched for reason, for sanity, for anything that could scatter the web spinning around them. "Why aren't you angry at Kim, at this whole thing? You were angrier with me for stepping into her place than you are with her. You hate scandal, remember, and this is only going to make you more interesting to the media."

"Kim's not eager to advertise her 'marriage'. And, until I have Emily's custody locked tight, I have you. Don't I?"

She couldn't understand how blithely he was handling the emotional aspect of this mess. He had to have felt something for Kim. *Didn't he?* "She left you for another man. Even for a man who rarely allows himself to feel anything, she did throw a kink in your plans for a perfect life."

A vein pulsed threateningly at his temple. "Why are you always so eager to find a weakness in me?"

"Anything is better than this unfeeling, ruthless man whom nothing touches. I hate that man."

His jaw clamped down. "Fine. I *am* angry with her. She risked everything I value. But, Kim and I, I think, were over long before I learned of her *wonderful* news."

Olivia couldn't control the shiver running through her. She licked her lips, and his gaze moved to her mouth, a gleam of something in it. Suddenly, he seemed feral, dangerous in a way she hadn't realized until now.

Being so drawn to her twin's man had been gut wrenchingly cruel, but there had been one strand of sanity that had shielded her from toppling all the way. Now there was nothing. Nothing to stop the deceitful hope mushrooming inside her. Nothing between her stupid heart and an abyss of pain.

The light blue dress shirt hugged the contours of his chest, the glimpse of curling chest hair through the opening drawing her gaze. She breathed and his tangy scent filled her. *When had he moved so unbearably close?* She dragged her gaze upward, the sexy slant to his mouth knocking the breath out of her. "Why didn't you tell me?"

His thumb moved over her jaw, toward her mouth. His upper lip curled. "Because I wanted to hold on to the illusion of control for a little longer."

Her breath hitched somewhere in her throat. She clasped his wrists to push him away, only he pulled her closer. Her breasts grazed his chest and she jerked, frissons of awareness coating her skin.

His gaze came alive with a lick of desire. And she shuddered from top to toe. Every breath she drew felt ragged, demanding, her whole body in a state of utter anticipation. "Alexander? Please don't."

His hand snaked around her waist, moved over her hip. He buried his mouth in the crook of her neck and smiled. "You minx," he breathed into her skin. "You deserve it for all the times you taunted me."

She moaned and threw her head back, the whisper of his hot mouth driving her wild. Her legs gave out under her. He dragged his lips upward in an openmouthed kiss that sent bolts of fiery need to her core.

She stared at him, at the tight, angular jaw, at the desire darkening his eyes to a dusky blue, arousal stamped onto every inch of his arresting features. His mouth descended on hers as her breath halted in her throat. Waves upon waves of sensation piled up inside as his lips brushed hers, soft and warm, testing, exploring. The taste of him sent erotic tingles through her body, all the way to her toes.

It was a moment she had imagined so many times, dreamed of, waking up tangled in her sweat-soaked sheets, aching and throbbing. But more than that, she had craved Alexander conceding to the desire between them, his dismissal of the attraction as something beneath him grating on her, while she absolutely lacked any kind of defense mechanism.

Her body thrummed with arousal, her nerves finely tuned strings, but she pushed him back, a monumental feat given her body craved only what he could give. "Why?"

He licked the seam of her mouth and she groaned.

"God, that's all I've wanted to do—"

His words were as potent as his kiss.

"Why was it over?" she said loudly, as if her words could pierce the haze of need enveloping her.

His lashes fanned down over his expression. His hands moved over her back, setting a fire over her bare skin. He gripped her hips and pulled her closer so that his erection rubbed against her belly. Her stomach quivered, her sex was clenched and tight, ready for what lay against her belly. She groaned as his hands moved over her breasts, his fingers brushing against their tight tips. "I need to look at you. I'm going to taste every inch of you."

It was blatant seduction to shut her up.

It felt unbearably good. His words sent erotic tingles rolling over her skin. Not that he didn't want her. The hard ridge of manhood under her palm, the groan that fell from his mouth as she rubbed herself against it was enough proof. But he was also using it to evade her...

She threw her head back as he kissed the birthmark on the slope of her breast, his tongue licking it, drawing circles around it. Her nipples tightened into almost-painful points, crying for the hot slide of his tongue. "That birth-mark has been driving me crazy."

She fought the spiral of desire sucking her downward, pushed her fingers up his nape into his hair and tugged hard. Until he was gazing into her eyes. The sculpted lines of his face more pronounced, his breathing harsh, he smiled, the dark amusement in his gaze winding her up. "If you like it rough," he rasped, his fingers equally tight on her nape. "I'll give it you, Liv. I will drive you to the edge until you're begging for release."

It felt so good to hold him like that, to feel her need mirrored in his tight, hard body. Because with every ragged breath, she knew that he was letting her do that, letting her hold on to the illusion that she was driving this, what-ever it was that was blazing between them. She shivered. She had never been so out of depth with a man as she was with Alexander. He could so easily unravel her. And the realization only spurred her on. "I want the truth," she said, and groaned as he cupped her butt and ground his arousal into her.

He tugged her lower lip with his teeth, sending frissons of sensations down her spine. She pushed him with the little strength she could muster. "Is it because she made a mistake? Because she disrupted your plans? Because—"

An almost pained sound erupted from his throat, a cross between a groan and a growl. *"Because you ruined every-thing."* She wanted the truth and it blazed out of his glitter-ing gaze. It glided over her skin, drowning every inch of her in it. "She's your twin. She *looks* like you. I can't look at her and not think of you. If I stayed with her, I would have to take her to my bed, have sex with her while all I can think of would be *you*." It was as if he was forcing himself to utter the very words he found so distasteful. "You think I'm so immune to everything that I'd have no problem with that?"

His admission spun around them, cocooning them in their own desires. It blasted the last of her defenses, rendering her immobile. There it was, everything she wanted to hear from him from the minute she had faced the inevitable truth of her own attraction. The words seeped into her blood, exploded behind her eyes, clogged her thinking.

His grip tightened over her hips and he lifted her onto the glass table. If there was even a semblance of control before, it was all gone now. She had asked for the truth and she had to pay the price now.

His gaze glittering with desire, he bent his head while his hand at her back held her. And sucked her nipple through the thin cotton. Her knees jelly, Liv sunk her hands into his hair, as he repeated the action. Arrows of pleasure zoomed straight to her sex and she clenched her thighs together.

He didn't let her. As though he could read her mind, his hands crept up her thighs under her dress, pushed the ridiculous thong she was wearing out of the way. She opened her mouth and gasped as his fingers parted her, and rubbed against her clitoris.

"Open your eyes and look at me," he ordered, his words gravelly.

She did. She would have done anything he asked of her at that moment. Need glittered in his blue gaze. He crushed her mouth with his again, his tongue caressing the insides. Putty in his hands, she didn't realize he had undone the knot at her neck until his tongue swiped over one rigid nipple while his fingers moved with sure intent over her sex, slow and fast. A million nerve endings stroked to life, she let out a throaty moan, her skin too hot and too tight. His clever fingers pulled, and stroked, and rubbed her tender flesh, she felt her muscles tighten, her breath stuck in her...

And suddenly he stopped.

She thought she would die. Until his long fingers teased her throbbing flesh again.

Every time she was close to her climax, every time she thought she would come apart, he slowed the pressure of his fingers, dragged his mouth upward to her neck until she fell from the dizzying heights he drove her to, frustrated and in sheer agony. Pleasure sizzled on her skin, quivered in her sex muscles, was so close that she could taste it on her tongue yet so far that she wondered if she would jump out of her skin. It was incredibly unfair, she thought in a haze, in a minute she would straighten, she would walk away...

Until he pushed a finger into her wet center and started the torment all over again. A swipe of his tongue over her nipple, there and yet gone in a second, a smooth glide of his thumb over her clit, enough but not enough...

"Oh..." she moaned, a sob rising in her throat. "You're..."

He laughed against the curve of her breast, his tongue licking erotic paths around the hard nipples aching for his touch. "Ask nicely, Olivia," he said, his words rolling over each other, his voice sounding drunk and hoarse.

She palmed his face and kissed him, the sinuous taste of him pulling her deeper. "Please, Alexander, I can't bear it..."

Just when she thought he would never stop punishing her, he pulled her nipple deep into his mouth. His teeth tugged at the hard nub while his fingers tightened on the exact place she needed them to.

She cried his name as her muscles contracted tight and released, her skin sizzled. Lights exploded behind her eyes, her body quaking and trembling.

He pulled her closer and pushed her hair from her forehead. He gently held her boneless body. His lips curved into a tight smile against her temple, his muscles under her hands bunched incredibly tight. "Now that I've touched you, I need to see you, taste you."

The most delicious shiver climbed up her spine at the dark promise in his words. She knew what he was doing. He was driving her crazy, pushing her to the edge, tormenting her for demanding the truth. She pulled his shirt out of his trousers and snuck her hands in. "No. I want touch you, too, I want to…"

Her words faltered as a knock sounded on the main door. A curse fell from his mouth and she laughed. His breathing rough and shallow, he leaned his forehead against her bare shoulder. The heat from his mouth singed her skin as he pressed an openmouthed kiss.

"Only Carlos could come knocking at the door right now. And he won't go away until I—" he said, regret lacing his words.

Liv nodded, her cheeks heating up, shying her gaze away from him. Suddenly, she felt inexplicably nervous.

She tugged the edges of her top upward and tied the knot at her nape. She jumped off the table just as Alexander returned with Carlos. His forehead creased into a frown, he looked anything but the man that had driven her to ecstasy mere minutes ago.

His hand over his nape, he walked around the living room, his movements anything but smooth. Did he even remember she was there? "How did she know where Emily was?"

"Who are you talking about?" Olivia said, before she could curb her tongue.

He glared at her, and she wondered if he would tell her to leave. He didn't. It was a measure of how much he had changed toward her. "Isabella persuaded Emily to leave with her from her vacation. But I had Carlos plant 24-7 security around Emily."

Sweat beaded on Olivia's brow as his words sunk in.

He hadn't said *tried to*...he had said *persuaded* like Emily had been ready to go. "Emily had been ready to leave?" she shot at Carlos.

Carlos remained silent. His silence said everything he didn't.

Alexander frowned. "That's not the point here, Liv."

She went to the fridge and took a bottle of water, trying to tune out their conversation. She needed to stay out of this, she *was* going to. She pressed the cold bottle to her heated cheeks, fighting to ignore the slow churn of anger in her gut.

"Let Isabella know that I will press kidnapping charges if she goes near Emily again." His words were cold, smooth and bare of anything. "And inform Emily's school that she's not returning."

Her fingers clenched around the bottle and she leaned her forehead against the cold, steel surface of the refrigerator.

She stayed like that, minutes after the door closed behind Carlos. The silence shifted and snarled between them. Her nape prickled as she felt Alexander behind her.

She stiffened as he laid an arm on her.

"Olivia, you're shaking." He pulled her toward him, his hard body behind her a deceptive invitation. Her muscles sighed against him, the evidence of his arousal electrocuting sense into her. She went into his arms like a rag doll as he turned her. "I'm going to regret asking this, aren't I?" He tilted her chin up. "What's wrong?"

Olivia closed her eyes, fighting for the strength to not care. And utterly failed. "How can you do this to her, to them?"

He clenched his jaw and released it. "Isabella will only bring misery to Emily. I can't let that happen."

An image of her mother, blurry, yet swamped in desperation, flashed in front of her eyes. The forgotten memory wrapped its choking fingers around her throat, clawing at her. "No, please, Alexander, listen. What if Isabella's changed? What if she's realized the value of what she's lost? Everyone deserves a second chance."

"You think I haven't given Isabella a chance? I have given her a million. Every time Nicholas hit her, I took care of her. I tried to shield her from his blows, I took them myself. I begged her to leave him, and every single time she promised me she would. And the fool that I was, I believed her. Until I realized one day that they were all lies.

"Do you want to know what happened the night she shot him? He smacked her across the face because she flirted with another man in front of him. When I stopped him, he kicked me in the gut. I was so angry. I grabbed the gun from her purse. I had only meant to scare him. To stop him. But Isabella grabbed it from me and fired it by accident. And even then, I hoped she would see how damaging their relationship was. I hoped that she would finally leave with me. And she didn't. She didn't care about me, what I did for her, how much I loved her. I meant nothing to her and it destroyed me to walk away, to let go, to fight the paralyzing hold my love for her had over me."

Tears spilled onto Olivia's cheeks. God, he had been barely seventeen. Not only had he gotten himself out, but he had taken on his sister. The anguish in his words, the pain in his eyes unraveled something inside her. No wonder he was so good at wiping away any emotion from his life, no wonder he didn't want to feel anything.

She stood up on her toes and hugged him for all she was worth. She peppered kisses over his granite jaw, touching him greedily, wishing she could take some of his pain away. His muscles shifted and shuddered beneath her hands, the emotion in him a minefield.

Alexander tugged Olivia to him and crushed her mouth. He didn't want to remember, didn't want to feel and it seemed only the taste of her could numb him, could close the gaping void he felt inside.

He didn't let her breathe. His hands in her hair, he kissed, nipped, bit her mouth until there was no more breath left in him, until he could feel nothing but the taste of her. But she didn't back off. She gave as good as she got, her ragged breathing a soothing sound to his ears. He laughed against her throat, as she ripped his shirt open, the buttons flying around them.

Olivia sighed. His skin felt like velvet coating hard rock to her touch, the muscles shifting and shuddering under her hands. She moved her hands lower and cupped him through his trousers, her mouth drying up.

He jerked back, his features set into stone. He leaned her forehead against hers and smiled. "God, it's going to kill me to stop this now, Liv, but I have to. I have to make sure Emily's okay. Wait up for me, okay?"

Olivia nodded, trying to even her breathing. She ran her hands over his chest again before pulling his shirt together. There was such an intimacy around the simple act that it cut through the sensual haze around her, straight to the matter that had her heart thumping. *What were they doing?* She swallowed and locked the question inside. "Maybe I could talk to Emily. She'll be angry with you, in fact, she'll hate you right now. I can talk to her and convince her that —"

"No," he said, his mouth wreaking havoc over her neck. "Don't interfere in this. Don't talk to Emily about Isabella, or yourself. In fact, I would appreciate it if you didn't say anything to Emily at all. I'm already taking a big risk by—" He licked where her pulse fluttered and she held on to him to stay upright. *Risk?* Thinking became hard when he touched her. "I can't risk anything else going wrong on top of Kim's news."

"I understand that but—"

"No, Liv. You need to stay out of this. If we want to see this crazy thing between us through, I need you to behave."

She flinched and stepped back. "Or what? You won't screw me?" Hurt seethed and boiled inside her, her stomach falling. "This is a first even for me, conditional sex."

Color swam into those razor sharp cheeks. "Don't cheapen it. That's not what I meant."

"No?"

A hard glint appeared in his eyes. "You have to know it can be nothing more than a fling, Liv, whatever this is between us."

"No, I don't know that. *'No casual sex for Alexander King.'* Wasn't that the headline when they voted you the perfect man? Every woman you dated, you did because you thought she could be the perfect woman, you had an equal relationship with them. Whereas with me, it seems you have automatically lowered your standards. Why's that, I wonder?"

He grabbed her and forced her to look into his blue eyes, scorching her with his gaze. "This is different. I've never done anything like—"

"Of course it is. Because I'm not good enough for anything other than sex and the pretense that I'm Kim, right?"

She tried to push him off but he didn't let her. "That's not what I think," he said hoarsely.

His grip on her was relentless until she gave up the fight and sagged against him, tears pooling in her eyes. Her gut felt as if it was turning on itself. "What were you thinking? Have me pretend to be Kim and screw me on the side until you had Emily's custody and then go looking for another perfect woman?"

His utter silence cut her open like a whiplash. Her chest hurt with every breath.

"You really are a heartless bastard. Only I forgot that for a while." She scrubbed her cheeks bitterly. "You know what? I'm actually going to take your advice. Take control and walk away. Because of all the mistakes I've made in my life, you would be the worst."

Alexander stood stunned as Olivia walked away, her spine ramrod straight. The raw pain in her eyes knocked the breath out of him, rendering him silent.

Would he have touched her, kissed her, if he had known that beneath that self-sufficiency, that defiant determination, Olivia was hurting? Was she right? Had he broken his own rules because somehow he had assumed that Olivia didn't deserve better?

Shame spiraled through him.

Every word he said, every action of his since he had met her, mocked him. Had he assumed he could sleep with her and then walk away with nothing changed?

He rubbed a hand over his eyes and stared at the door. Even now, the need to walk into that room and take what he wanted, to promise her anything just so that he could wipe the grief from her eyes was feral. But he couldn't, not if he wanted to face himself in the mirror tomorrow morning.

He had to limit the damage to his life.

He had to walk away from Olivia before the havoc she wreaked on him, the pain *he* caused her, became something that he could never undo.

CHAPTER TEN

OLIVIA THANKED THE flight attendant, leaned back into the luxurious leather seat and took a sip of her coffee. In the seat opposite her, dressed in a severely cut Ralph Lauren dress, Emily King sat rigid, the tension from her lanky frame swathing them all. There was such a depth of sadness in her gaze that Olivia couldn't look away.

Ever since she had arrived at Alexander's penthouse this morning, mere hours before they had boarded the flight, Emily had attacked Alexander with a savage anger. And more surprising was Alexander's infinite patience with his sister. Amid Emily's continuous barbs and tantrums, he had been nothing but incredibly gentle.

A chill crawled up Liv's spine.

Watching Emily was like looking in the mirror and seeing her most self-destructive version, even if she hadn't known it then. Confused, starved for attention, willing to go to any lengths. With every passing minute, it was becoming harder and harder to keep her mouth shut.

"We've been over this, Emily." Alexander sighed as Emily, once again, refused anything to eat. "Starving yourself won't get you anywhere."

Her blue gaze, so much like her brother's, glittered with determination. "No, but it hurts you, doesn't it? And right now, that's all I care about."

Olivia gasped at the bitterness in the teenager's tone. Could Alexander not see that she was a train-wreck waiting to happen?

Every instinct within her wanted to help the girl, maybe even grab her and run once they landed in New York, before Alexander's rigid constraints pushed Emily into doing something reckless.

Because Olivia would bet her last precious dollar that the teenager wasn't going to meekly obey.

She set her coffee cup down and cleared her throat. "May I speak with you, Emily?"

"Stay out of this, Liv," Alexander roared at her.

"You're Olivia, not Kim," Emily instantly caught on, her gaze studying Liv curiously.

Liv nodded, smiling as Alexander's muted curse reached her ears.

A tentative smile curved Emily's mouth, her anger at her brother momentarily forgotten. "I've heard so much about you at school. My friends and I think you are the coolest. Everyone's always talking about how you broke so many of those stupid rules, I mean, you were even expelled because you—" Pink flushing her angular cheeks, Emily pursed her mouth, her gaze anxious. "Sorry, I didn't mean to… How did you end up with Alex of all people?"

Olivia sighed. Really, how equipped was she to dish out advice to a confused teenager? To actually think, she had indulged, even if for a crazy second, that she could steal Emily away from Alexander's care. "That's a long story, Emily."

Alexander's wrath next to her was a tangible thing. Even Emily looked anxiously from him to her. "The last thing Emily needs is a talk with—"

"And once again, I don't care what you think," Liv burst out. Their gazes collided, tension spiraling tighter and tighter. "What will you do? Cut me out of your life if I don't behave? Oh, wait, you would have already done that except you need me."

Alexander glared at her. "Don't push it, Liv. You've already gotten yourself kicked out of a project to work on and who knows what's next. You know more than anyone—"

"How ruthless you can be?" she finished, her insides trembling. "Yes."

Emily's laugh reverberated around them. "Wow, I like you already."

Olivia ran shaking fingers through her hair. This was *so* not what she had intended when she had opened her mouth. She leaned forward in her seat. "I understand how much you want to see your mother. I can even imagine all the ways you're scheming to get in touch with her once you're in New York. My punishment when I didn't stop talking about my mom was to be packed off to boarding school, too. I hated my father so much for that."

Right on cue, the color leached from Emily's face. "Then you know how much I—"

"I do. But please don't do something you'll regret for the rest of your life, Emily. Once you go down that path, there's no—"

"I don't need another adult preaching me." Tears filled her blue gaze. "All I want is to see my parents."

Olivia clutched the girl's hand, memories she didn't want to remember swarming her, the helpless, stifling feeling that had been a constant companion. Every decision made for her, every choice taken out of her hands, from something as trivial as dancing classes that she'd hated, to something as important as what she remembered about her own mother.

Every nerve in her wanted to help Emily escape. Because, Alexander would never give his mother another chance. Instead, she forced herself to concentrate on how much she had regretted her own actions when it had been too late.

"I understand, I really do. But there's a fundamental difference between you and me." She struggled to speak through the lump in her throat. "Your brother might be an arrogant, controlling ass but he loves you. I've no doubt about that.

"If I had had someone who truly loved me like that, I like to think my life would have turned out differently." Olivia smiled through the tears clogging up her vision, at the void opening up inside her. Her heart wept for the teenager she had been, for the girl who had never had the chance. "That I wouldn't have made a mess out of it like I have. And you do. I'm not asking you to let Alexander walk all over you, but don't do something that will ruin your life to get back at him."

She moved to the seat next to Emily and huddled toward her. She had no idea if anything she had said made sense to the younger girl, but Liv was damned if she let Alexander browbeat her into not caring. Especially in the coming days, knowing what Alexander had planned for her, Emily was going to need a friend. "Tell you what. How about anytime you need to blow steam, or have an I-hate-Alexander-King session, you call me?"

A smile split Emily's mouth, and Olivia swallowed. She looked beyond Emily to Alexander, the pregnant silence from him sending a shiver up her spine. Their gazes met and held, her chest hurting with each breath she pulled in.

"Believe it or not, I'm the founding member of that club," she said, wondering when, if ever, her heart would learn.

Olivia thanked the receptionist on the ground floor of King Towers and walked toward the seating area, the tap-tap of her high-heeled boots an echo in her ears. She checked her reflection in the gleaming coffeepot as she poured herself a cup. A neat French plait held her unruly hair back. A white dress shirt added the touch of professionalism she needed to add to her unconventional long skirt and leather boots.

Her stomach a jumble of knots, she smoothed the non-existent creases out of her black skirt. After everything that had happened with Alexander, she'd almost given up. She had done that before, had let her personal life, her impulses cloud her professional judgment.

For the first time in her life, she had come fully prepared, worked her backside off to be ready. And had worked ten times harder to convince Nate that she should be allowed to pitch.

She had used every bit of logic at her disposal to achieve it. LifeStyle Inc. and by extension, King Enterprises' flawless reputation for fair business practices, which really had been the easy part seeing that Nate was obsessed with Alexander's immaculate reputation and business acumen, and her own efforts in the past six months to forge herself a career, how hard she had worked on the presentation, how she was the one best equipped to make it a success, it had been little short of begging.

And the more she had tried to convince him, the more she had realized the truth in Alexander's words. She had been too ready to give in, to walk away. Only the need to prove him wrong had fueled her willpower. He must have known how his disparaging words would motivate her.

She was ushered inside a vast conference room. She connected her laptop to the screen and checked her settings. A huge rectangular table stood at the other end. She opened a bottle of water from the side table, and took a drink. She switched on the remote and her presentation appeared on the screen.

One by one, a few executives, all dressed in identical black suits, entered the room. A bead of sweat ran between her shoulder blades as she scanned each face, her stomach twisting on itself. She had worked hard to get here and she wasn't going to let anyone derail her.

The glass door clicked open, and she turned, steeling herself.

She clutched the edge of the dark oak table, her knuckles turning white at her grip. Her heartbeat notched up, sick fear lodging into her throat.

The man who walked in was not Vincent Gray. She mustered a smile as he introduced himself as Daniel Adams.

Her jaw slackened, a rush of gratitude and something else, something she didn't even want to acknowledge rose up inside her. For a few interminable seconds, she just stood there, as he settled into the last chair in the center of the group.

"I thought we would be pitching to Mr. Gray."

The newcomer spoke up. "Mr. Gray resigned recently. Do you want to begin, Ms. Stanton?"

Nodding absently, Olivia turned sideways and looked at her presentation. For a horrifying minute, the screen looked jumbled. She took a deep breath and focused on how much she had overcome to be here.

Shutting out everything else, she began highlighting their campaign. Within minutes, she found her stride, excitement a huge ball in her stomach. She was halfway through when she was interrupted.

"We're launching a sportswear line, products to be used by men and women interested in outdoor activities, and your primary campaign tool is Twitter. Does anyone else see the problem here?"

Olivia could feel the color flushing into her face. "Yes, but—"

"We're not just launching a new sportswear line," Daniel said. "We want people to think of our clothes, our gear, as synonymous of a new lifestyle. So the campaign for it should spur people into action, into living their life instead of talking about it on their computers."

Olivia smiled, excitement thrumming in her veins. It was exactly what her campaign was designed to do. "And to do that you have to use social media," she piped in, clicking through to the next slide. "What our agency is proposing is a twenty-first century treasure hunt, sort of a Twitter driven *Amazing Race*. We'll have the usual advertising through television and billboards, but you'll lose a big chunk of your audience if you neglect social media. We start in a city like New York, feed clues online for a treasure hunt in a National park, for the prizes—the new gear you're selling, hidden all over the city. Soon LifeStyle Inc. will be on the mouth of every teenager, every woman or man who has ever been on a social media site."

She didn't give them a break. She continued talking through the campaign, gaining more and more confidence with the intelligent questions thrown her way. By the end of the allotted two hours, she felt as though she had run a marathon herself. She handed the folders that detailed the campaign to all the members. A couple of the men congratulated her on their way out on the innovativeness of the campaign. Her mouth dry, she shook Daniel's hand and answered some more questions.

"You're the last agency on our shortlist, Ms. Stanton. I'm confident enough in my board to say your campaign provides exactly the kind of exposure we want. Congratulations. We will contact your agency with our final decision in a few days."

Olivia held her tears back through sheer will until the room emptied. She had done it. She had found something she was good at, achieved something through her own talent.

She tugged her laptop bag onto her shoulder, dying to

get back to the office and give Nate all the details. She was going to celebrate her achievement tonight, she wasn't going to let one man ruin it.

CHAPTER ELEVEN

ALEX BROUGHT HIS BMW to a smooth halt and killed the engine. The neighborhood had started giving into grunge a few blocks back. A slow burn of anger rose through him with each graffitied house and run-down apartment complex he passed.

He'd known Olivia was broke, he'd read Carlos's report that she lived in a run-down neighborhood along the outer fringes of Manhattan. But it hadn't prepared him for the sight of it. Her little studio was on the fourth floor of an apartment building whose best feature was that it looked clean.

It felt as if a hammer was pounding incessantly behind his eyes. He had just flown back from Abu Dhabi after a week of nonstop meetings.

His eyes felt like sand was coated into them, he hadn't had a decent night's sleep in he didn't know how long. If he thought about this using his head, as he was known to do, he shouldn't be here. The increased frequency of Isabella's phone calls, Emily's incessant questions and his decision to get Emily's custody sorted soon rather than later—his personal life was in the worst shape for the first time in twelve years. Yet, all he could think of, all he could see in his mind's eye was Olivia's pale face, the hurt shimmering in her huge eyes.

How could he let her go on believing the worst about herself?

His nape prickling, he watched in absolute shock as he recognized the man stepping out of her building. *What was Carlos doing here?* He was out of the car before he could blink and crossed the road. His heart beat an incessant tattoo, his mind running through so many different scenarios.

He came to a halt in front of Carlos. "Carlos, is she—"

"She's fine. She had a little incident with the press and fell."

Of course she did. Thinking you had everything in control when Olivia Stanton featured in your life was a very big mistake. Alexander circled his nape and pressed with his fingers, feeling an invisible knot tighten there. "Where the hell were you?"

Carlos and he'd known each other for fifteen years. Alex trusted him more than anyone else, which was why he'd asked him to keep an eye on Olivia.

His head of security eyed him with the same remote look he leveled at everyone. "I was bringing the car around to pick her up and asked her to wait," he muttered, running a hand through his overlong hair. "Even though they see her as 'Olivia', working for you is drawing enough attention. I was gone for two minutes. By the time I was back, she walked into the mob and one of them shuffled her until she fell."

Alexander kicked a pebble with all the force he could muster and let loose a string of expletives that felt very true to the neighborhood. He stepped toward the entrance, only to have Carlos's muscular frame block him. He rubbed his temple with his fingers, feeling his nerves tautly stretched, every muscle in him itching for a fight. "Spit it out, Carlos."

"This isn't you, Alex." Carlos looked as if he was struggling for the right words, which surprised Alex even more.

"You have more integrity, more discipline than any man I've ever known. Don't play with that girl knowing that you'll only break her in the end."

Alex stood there for a few minutes as Carlos left without a backward glance, the thick silence of the night cloaking him. In all the years he had worked for him, Carlos had never commented on his personal life. Yet a few days with Olivia, and he was already her champion.

Olivia pulled her T-shirt down, its length hitting her midthigh, and squeezed the water out of her hair. Her head throbbed. She looked on the counter for the painkillers she had been given and sighed. She had left them in Carlos's car. She could go to the drugstore around the corner but she had no energy tonight to chat with either seventy-year-old Mrs. Robbins or the twenty-year-old self-proclaimed stud Pinto.

She ran a tentative hand over her forehead, and winced as her fingers grazed the gauze dressing. Just her luck that she had to fall on a scrap of metal wire that meant she had needed stitches. She took a sip from the bottle of wine that Nate had given her and scrunched her nose in distaste. *Just great.* Now her palette was too spoiled for cheap wine. But it didn't mean it wouldn't get her sloshed pretty good.

She had had a hell of a week and a half. She had worked fourteen-hour days, going over the contract details and budgeting with Daniel and Nate. It had been the hardest working week of her life. It was exactly the way she wanted it.

Stupidly, she had hoped that she might see Alexander again on her many trips to King Towers. Every time a tall man with broad shoulders had passed by her stomach had dived. Until she'd realized what small potatoes LifeStyle Inc. was in Alexander's business empire. Of course there had been no sight of him. She finally had stopped looking when she'd heard someone mention that he was out of the country.

Which was for the best. It was easier to hate him, be angry with him at a distance, to assure herself that he had no power over her, that the time she had spent with him in Paris had left no mark on her.

Self-delusion—1, bitter reality—0.

The doorknob rattled from the outside. "Go away, Pinto," she yelled. The fiddling didn't stop. Her heart in her mouth, she turned around when the door was pushed through and Alexander walked in.

She sank onto her bed, her knees trembling. "You broke the lock!"

A look of pure rage crossed his features, tight lines fanning around his mouth. "You call that a lock?" He pushed the door shut behind him with a grunt, the thud shaking everything in sight. "I didn't even have to put my weight on it. Do you know that there's a weirdo outside in the corridor peeking at your door without blinking? And you're walking around dressed in that," he muttered through gritted teeth, "flimsy little thing."

Liv stared at him with her mouth hanging open. "Pinto's absolutely harmless."

"No one's harmless in New York. He could…do anything to you and no one would know."

While he ranted and raged around her, she took the opportunity to simply look at him, starved for the sight of him. There was a hint of stubble to his jaw, a sunken, haggard look to his eyes. Yet nothing punctured the potency of his presence. She tucked her hands at her sides, every muscle in her quivering to touch him, to feel his solid strength with her hands.

She raised her gaze and met his, the scorching naked hunger in it robbing the breath from her. Her skin prickled with awareness, jolts of desire, hot as lava, sparking off every inch of her. For long, taut moments, they stood like that, staring at each other.

"Get dressed, we're leaving."

She jerked her head, wondering if she heard him right. "Not only did you break the lock on my door, you're ordering me around now? The landlord will raise my rent again." *Was the man going to ruin everything for her?* She shivered as a breeze flew in through the window. "You're not the boss of me, at least not directly," she added, as a gleam entered his eyes, "so get out."

He didn't say anything. Just maneuvered his tall, lean frame to the narrow counter and stove, which was technically her kitchen. He opened the cupboards above the counter, and the refrigerator, his movements rough and frustrated with each passing second.

He was standing there like he'd every right to, looking down upon her home, ordering her around, chipping away the wall of hurt and anger she had built up.

She did need the word *stupid* tattooed on her forehead.

She turned around and folded her hands, striving for a calm she wasn't feeling. Dark color slashed his sharp-angled cheekbones, and her nipples instantly puckered, rasping against the thin material of her tee. "What?" She spat out the word, nothing more coherent coming to her aid.

He loomed over her, a giant, mobile wall of anger. "You have no food, a creep outside that door, you might have a concussion and you're getting—" she winced as he cursed "—drunk. You're a hazard to yourself."

"Not that I've to explain myself to you, but I've been taking care of myself for a long time."

She swallowed as his gaze swept over her breasts. When had he moved so close that she could see the dark shadow of his skin under the white shirt, that she could smell the hint of spice in his cologne enough to buckle her knees?

He raised his hand and ran his long fingers over the graze on her cheek. "And look how well that worked out for you."

Her breath hitched in her throat.

His mouth was a tight line as he studied the gauze, as if he'd waited on purpose before he acknowledged that she was hurt. "Why didn't you wait for Carlos, Olivia?" His fingers trembled over her skin. "You know what rabid dogs they can be."

She did. But she had been so angry and she still couldn't get over how vicious they had been. She shouldn't have drawn their interest at all. She had spent the past six months doing everything she could to maintain a low profile, except for the small incident with Vincent. Yet they had come after her just because of her connection to Alexander. His obsession over his privacy made so much sense now. "They just swarmed me as I was leaving King Towers. I'm not even… Anyway, I wanted to hit one idiot. You should see this one. He'll put the whole horde that hounds you to shame. I can proudly say I've provided this particular scumbag with a livelihood so far. But of course, he couldn't just let me be, he has to put a spin on everything that happens in my life."

His gaze flickered to hers. "What did he say?"

She tried to even out the hurt from her tone. "He asked me how I was enjoying the success that was bestowed upon me by my brother-in-law."

"You couldn't ignore it and walk away?" He sounded ragged, at the end of his rope. "Why do you act on every impulse that runs through your head?"

"Why do you care?" She pushed the words through a throat raw with hurt and longing. She was slowly losing the strength to fight him, to fight this. Every argument with him eroded her decision to keep her distance, every little flash of concern beneath his cutting indifference knocked off a little more of her resistance. "Why are you here, Alexander?"

A huge sigh rattled his body, and he sank to her tiny bed. He tugged her down and she scooted over to keep a little distance between them. His long legs stuck out in front of him as he planted them on an old armchair. He pushed his hair back with his fingers, and held his head in them. "There's something I need to tell you. And I—" she turned her head, giving into the urge to just look at him; his jaw was locked tight "—wanted to see you."

She felt as though her heart would explode out of her chest. She clutched her middle, a shiver running through her. "Don't do this. I—"

He reached up, his thumb moved over her mouth, silencing her. "I couldn't let you go on believing that what I wanted between us, the casual thing...that it had to be that way because it was you," he said, his words harsh and tense. "You should give yourself more credit, Liv. And that's just not when it comes to your career." The tenderness in his gaze undid her. "You deserve the best any man can give."

Olivia trembled at the impact of his words, a river of dizzy joy flushing her from within. Her legs folded under her, her heart bursting into speed. "Then why?"

"Isn't it enough that I'm saying it, Liv?" He turned away from her. "You're the most resilient, most courageous woman I've ever met."

"Please, Alexander. I deserve the truth."

"It's not you. It's how I react to everything about you. It's the power you have over me." Olivia's heart jumped into her throat. He sounded guttural, like the admission was wrung out of him under promise of pain. "I don't have control over myself with you. I lose all rationality. I don't know myself, I'm capable of anything, everything. I become the worst of myself and I loathe it."

It destroyed me to walk away, to let go, to fight the paralyzing hold my love for her had over me.

Olivia shivered at the memory of his words as realization slithered through her, both crushing and freeing, like the roller coaster that took her on a dizzying high at the price of the downward spiral. What she was was what drew Alexander to her and what he felt for her would be what would drag him away.

A pang of something shot through her, leaving her giddy and pained in equal measures. She felt a fist squeezing her chest, a sudden chill grabbing hold of her, and everything blurred for a second. The heartbreaking, breath-robbing, gut-clenching truth was that she was falling for him.

And she didn't know how to stop it, there was no parachute to slow the descent, only the utterly terrifying truth that it would end with her heart crushed into so many pieces.

There was no happily ever after for her. Because this man who stared at her with incredible desire in his beautiful eyes, who felt something for her but abhorred the fact that he did, he was *it* for her.

Because no one could hold a candle to Alexander, no one would even come near scratching the surface of what she felt for him today, and despite all his efforts to deny it, to crush everything, no one would understand her, no one would love her better than he did.

Every inch of her trembled and shuddered as he tugged her hand into his. He kissed the sensitive spot on her wrist, his mouth a searing brand. "I can't get you out of my mind. I want to touch you, I want to kiss you and I want to cover every inch of your skin with mine. And I've reached the end of my rope. Tell me to leave, tell me to get the hell out of your life. Because I can't promise you anything, I can't give you what you deserve."

She wanted to move away from him, to hold on to a little

sanity. But she couldn't. If she sent him away, she would never see him again. Because whatever he claimed, he was a man of integrity. He would never speak of this again.

The thought sent waves of nauseating panic prickling over her skin. How could she deny herself the chance to be with him?

Winning the advertising contract for her agency, proving to herself that she was more than her choices, that she could succeed at something, they were all things she had needed. And she had them now. But couldn't she change the fundamental part of her that felt so much.

She couldn't let him walk away.

She inched forward and pressed her mouth to the corner of his. Heat blasted inside her, every inch of her seeking, crying for his touch, for his caresses.

His hands moved to her shoulders, but he didn't press her toward him, or touch her except to anchor her. In fact, after a couple of seconds, she realized he wasn't even kissing her. He just stilled, his heart racing under her fingers, a shudder coursing through him. And he wouldn't kiss her unless she asked him now, unless she made a decision.

The scent of him beneath his cologne sent a wave of longing through her.

She pressed her mouth to his, fully this time. His lips were hard and soft at the same time, sending a sweeping roar of longing through her. His powerful body racked as a shudder went through him. "Please don't go, Alexander."

CHAPTER TWELVE

HIS HAND SNAKED around her nape, into her hair and pulled her close, while the other cupped her cheek. "You're going to make this as hard as possible, aren't you?"

"What do you mean?"

His hands traveled up her arms, his fingers moving over her skin in mesmerizing circles, as if he couldn't help it after holding back for so long. She trembled all over when his hands reached her shoulders, and pressed slightly. The thin material of her tee was no barrier to the heat gliding from his touch to her skin. His long fingers moved to her neck, tilted her head up to meet his gaze.

She moved her hands to his chest, encountering hard muscle that sent jolts of awareness through her fingers. His heart rumbled under her hands.

"It doesn't matter," he said, sliding his hot mouth over her jaw, to the pulse at her neck. She shivered as he licked her skin. He pulled back and stood at the edge of the bed, his gaze never wavering from her.

He tugged his tie loose, and yanked it away. "Take off that T-shirt."

She froze at the raw desire in his tone, his hoarse command setting her skin ablaze with need. There was a razor-edged calm to his movements, a dark shadow in his gaze, as if he didn't give a damn anymore, as if, now that they were giving into it, there was no need even for the facade of control, for the veil of restraint.

It terrified her and aroused her at the same time.

His fingers worked feverishly on the buttons of his shirt. He chucked it off, his lean, tightly muscled chest stealing the remaining air from her lungs. She watched him, her mouth dry, unable to move, unable to speak, the taut rippling of his chest muscles as his hands moved to his trousers, and stilled as his gaze took in her frozen stance. "You have five seconds to change your mind, Liv."

Her nipples hardened, the soft cotton of her tee chafing against them. She shook her head, enjoying the sight of him too much to even muster a response. His gaze never moved from her, as he rid himself of his trousers and boxer shorts.

She didn't turn away, she didn't even blink, she couldn't if her life depended on it. Broad shoulders narrowed down to a lean waist and leaner hips. A smattering of dark hair disappeared into a line down his washboard stomach. Even the muscles at his groin were well formed, sending a blaze of heat over her.

She licked her lips, and his erection, thick and jutting up, twitched at the innocent movement. Her breaths came hard and fast, dampness pooled at her core. She needed to touch him. She extended a shaky hand toward him as he reached the bed. Her fingers grazed the velvety hardness of his shaft but he stopped her, his fingers wrapping around her wrist.

"No."

With that word, he grabbed her hands and hitched them over her head. And then he climbed into the bed, looming over her like a dark shadow, pressing her into the bed. Her bed creaked under his weight. The meager light from the overhead bulb threw the hard planes of his face into sharp relief.

She wanted to protest, wanted to say something as he

pushed her back. But then he slid his huge body, a hard wall of heat, over hers, until he covered every inch of her, just as he'd said. Their mingled moans rent the air. Her breasts were crushed against the solid wall of his chest, his erection skimmed her belly and his rock-hard thighs cradled her groin. The most delicious feeling crept into her already sluggish blood.

He raised his head and met her gaze, something flickering in it. She felt a curious urge to shy her gaze away from him, never having mastered the art of hiding her feelings. She felt naked, devoid of armor, a curious vulnerability she had never experienced before. His free hand moved, palm downward, drawing a path upward over the thin material of her tee, touching, not touching, throwing her headlong into a spiral of need.

She panted, fighting for breath as he buried his face at the base of her neck and inhaled deeply. Her tummy rolled on itself as he licked the spot, her fingers threading around his biceps. She wanted to pull him to her, she wanted to touch him, wanted him to touch her properly—all the achy, needy places crying for his attention, yet she couldn't get her arms to understand her intent.

She felt his mouth curve against her skin, his hot open-mouthed kiss singeing her flesh. She shivered all over. He shifted his weight a little to the side. "Of all the times to be scared, now, Liv?"

She moaned as he tugged her tee off one shoulder and sank his teeth into her flesh. She inched her fingers over his nape, into his hair and tugged his face up. The tendons in his neck stood to attention, the angles of his cheekbones jutting out. "I'm fine."

"Good, because I can't do this slowly."

His voice sounded drugged, so unlike him that she stared at him, whatever she had been thinking a forgotten mist in her head. He rolled her tee up, color bleeding into his cheekbones with each inch of her flesh he uncovered. Her skin, in turn, tingled with sensation, prickled with need. His hands faltered for a split second when he inched the cotton over her breasts, his gaze riveted to them. And then he pulled the tee over her head. Before she could blink, he tugged her panties down over her boneless legs.

"Protection?"

With his stubble grazing the side of her breast, it took her a second to grasp his meaning. She wanted to squeeze her legs together, but he lay in between them, his erection a hard, pulsing weight rubbing against her groin. "Pill," she answered, glad that she didn't have to say more than one word.

"Perfect, because I need to be—" he pulled at her ankle and placed her leg over his shoulder, his erection rubbed against her core and she groaned restlessly, her skin too tight, too hot to bear "—inside you *now*."

Balancing his weight on his elbows, he entered her in one deep thrust. Their combined moans, guttural and needy, shook the air as he filled her completely. A sense of utter completion filled her as he laid his face in the crook of her neck, his breaths coming hard and fast, his chest crushing her breasts. His stubble was rough against her skin, his muscles hard against hers. His shoulders were like a steel wall under her fingers. Yet it felt painfully good, beyond anything she'd imagined.

She opened her eyes and froze at the stark beauty of the man. Every muscle in his body, from his spectacular face to the lean strength of his shoulders, looked as if it was carved from granite, a study in masculine perfection. He rose above her, his weight on his elbows, his back arched, every muscle, every sinew stretched with tension. "I can't not move," he muttered, a depth of regret in his gaze.

With that hoarse statement, he pulled out all the way, slowly, letting her feel every inch of him, and thrust back into her with a force that would have sent her to the top of the bed if he hadn't held her anchored to him, exactly where he needed her to be.

She cried out, at the friction, at the hot quiver of her muscles, at the ache slowly building up over her lower belly, at the need spiraling inside her as he repeated the action. His pelvis rocked against hers with each thrust, pushing her a little higher on the bed. His movements were rough, fast, her cheap bed creaking every time he moved.

And it was exactly what she wanted from him. Because he had thrown off the last vestiges of control, because he was giving into what he wanted and it was the Alexander she loved, the Alexander she wanted.

She raised her bottom and met him halfway on his next thrust, sensation upon sensation piling upon her, every nerve ending blasted into a higher plane where only pleasure existed. He cursed, long and hard, drops of sweat beading his forehead, a delicious tension in every inch of him.

She moaned, the sound clawing its way up her throat, as he rubbed the pad of his palm over her cleft, almost-painful pleasure splintering into a thousand fragments within her, the muscles of her core contracting and expanding, her body jumping out of her frayed skin. She dug her nails into his back as he thrust deeper and harder one last time, his body a taut wire. And then he was shuddering, his grunt, guttural and hoarse, as he spilled into her and collapsed over her.

He was crushing her, her breathing already fractured and uneven. But she couldn't protest, couldn't even say a word. It felt so good to be lying beneath him, it hurt so much that he would walk away from this that she felt a dark void of pain open up in her gut. She shut her eyes, scared that he would see too much.

Slowly, he shifted away from her. Olivia fisted her

hands into the sheets. It was either that or grab him with both hands so that he couldn't move away from her.

But he didn't.

He moved to the side on her tiny bed and tugged her closer when she'd have shuffled away. He pulled the throw over them, encasing them in warmth. But nothing could take away the chill that had already seeped into her blood. "Liv," he said, pushing away her sweat-slicked hair from her forehead, a tremor coloring his voice like she'd never heard before, "please, look at me."

Olivia opened her eyes. A hint of uncertainty gleamed in the depths of his eyes. "Are you okay? I didn't—"

Her smile cost her more effort than anything else. She didn't want his gentleness, that was the one thing that would break the wave of mounting grief she was holding inside. "I'm perfectly fine."

He dipped his mouth toward her and crushed her lips to his, as if he couldn't get close enough. The feel and taste of his mouth pervaded into her blood. He touched his forehead to hers, his breath mingling with hers. A bleakness she'd never seen before entered his gaze. "You see what I am when I'm with you." His sigh shook her. "I've never taken a woman like that, Liv, without foreplay, so roughly, so selfishly, as though nothing mattered except possession."

Olivia moved her hands over his, leaning in when he kissed her palm. She ran her hands over his chest, greedy for contact, raking a finger over a hard nipple. "You did nothing I didn't want, Alexander."

She wanted to tell him that she didn't care, but the words froze on her lips.

He wore no mask, he was at the mercy of his needs, desires, he didn't or couldn't erect a wall around his emotions when he was with her. He was not the perfect man the world thought him. He lost control, he hurt and he was someone who needed her as much as she needed him, even if he didn't admit that.

But the realization warmed and chilled her blood. Because whatever made this thing between them so real, so good, was also what was going to keep him away from her. Because Alexander was never going to embrace the part of him that felt, that hurt, the part that he had suppressed to survive. And she was fooling herself if she thought she could change that.

Tears stung behind her eyes, but she forced them back. She pressed her mouth to his jaw and dragged it toward his mouth. She bit his lower lip, and he moaned. The sound sent a tingle straight to her core. Tomorrow was going to come soon enough. Tonight, she didn't want to think. "Now, please…"

The words trailed away from her mouth as he snuck his hand between their bodies, and pressed a finger into her core, while his thumb rubbed her clitoris in mind numbing circles. "Please, what?"

She threw her head back and groaned, coils of sensation gripping her lower belly again. She moved her hands over his torso, and snuggled a little closer. "I don't want to talk, I don't want to think. Just do something, anything."

Plunging his hands into her hair, he tugged her upward, and plundered her mouth. He didn't wait to be invited into her mouth this time, sucking and biting her lips. He tugged her lower lip between his teeth and pressed his advantage when she gasped. She met him, move to move, until their mouths were fused together, biting, sucking, licking. And she still didn't get enough.

He dragged his mouth to her neck, his breathing harsh, while his hands roamed hungrily over her midriff. "This time I'm taking it slow even if it kills me." He tracked a trail of kisses to her ear. "What would you like me to do next, Liv?"

With her hands in his hair, she tugged his head back, until they were both staring into each other's eyes, the sound of their fractured breathing buffeting them. "Touch my breasts, please. I will die if you don't."

It was all the persuasion Alexander needed. He cupped her breasts, molding them with his hands, running the pads of his thumbs over their hard peaks. He flicked one swollen pink peak with the tip of his finger, and she pushed herself into his touch with a strangled moan. He pushed the words out through a dry mouth, the sight of his dark fingers on her pink nipples incredibly erotic. "You have the sexiest nipples. Pink, and tight and ripe, just begging to be sucked. Would you like that, Liv?"

She nodded frantically, and Alexander smiled. "Yes. And I'll kill you if you stop now."

He wrapped his hands at her waist, bent his head and pulled one hard tip into his mouth, and sucked.

Olivia bucked against his hands, an arrow of sensation zooming straight through to her core. She thrust her hands into his hair and held on tight as he shifted his attention to the other breast and suckled at it. Her guttural moan echoed around them when he tugged the nipple with his teeth. Need clawed inside her skin. She moved closer to him, needing more, the ache between her legs intensifying with every pull of his wicked mouth.

"Turn around," he ordered and she meekly did. She was putty in his hands and she had no intention or strength to resist.

He dropped a kiss between her shoulders, and she shivered. He held her hands over them with one hand, while the other one drew a line down her spine, followed by his hot mouth and erotic tongue. He reached the indent above her buttocks and stopped. The mattress groaned as he shifted to switch on the bedside lamp, still holding her down. Only then did she realize that he was staring at her tattoo.

She turned her head sideways, trying to get a look at him.

A strip of color darkened his cheeks. Silence enveloped them as he ran the pad of his thumb over the butterfly tattoo, up and down, sending little sparks of need shooting through to the aching, wet spot between her legs, making her weak-kneed.

She licked her lips. She hated herself for asking, for wanting his approval but did it, anyway. "Don't you like tattoos?"

Alexander looked up as Olivia's tentative voice penetrated the red haze clouding his mind. A surge of emotion washed through him and he took a deep breath, trying to fight it down, to clamp down. To no avail. He ran his thumb over the alluring tattoo again, despising himself for the possessiveness that settled in his gut, jealousy an acidic taste on his tongue. "It's very sensuous," he murmured, clearing his throat.

A smile tugged the corners of his mouth. Her chin tilted at a defiant angle, her eyes blazing. "Meaning what exactly?"

"Meaning it suits you perfectly, Olivia," he repeated, uncaring that a harsh note entered his tone. But then, it was the first time he was experiencing something so irrational, so elemental that he had no idea how to react to it. His reaction was petty, beneath him. Yet the fact that another man would have seen the tattoo, another man would have kissed the alluring flesh let loose a beast inside him.

Things he had no right to ask, things he *shouldn't* even want to know, gnawed at him. The women he'd dated had been intelligent, successful women who had no qualms about their sex life. Yet he had never felt this curious about their pasts, this irrational jealousy over men they had shared their bodies with. This was what she did to him, what she evoked in him, things no confident, decent man would think. She reduced him into nothing.

Olivia didn't know what had changed but something had and not for the good. A hardness entered Alexander's gaze, transforming the tenor of the very air around them into something dark. "If you don't like—"

Her words were lost in her gasp as he plundered her mouth again. She moaned against his mouth and he swooped in, flicking her tongue with his, tasting and exploring every inch of her mouth until they were both moaning with ragged need, until she had no idea where he began and where she ended. Sliding between her parted lips, he stroked her to ecstasy with his tongue, darting in and out of her mouth, an erotic act in itself and she clenched her hands on his shoulders, her nails digging into his skin. He was using every skill at his disposal to drive her crazy.

He moved his free hand to the curls between her legs. But she wanted control this time, even if it lasted only a few minutes.

She pushed his hand away and in a quick movement, surprised him until he lay on his back. There was only so much she could endure in his wicked hands. With a laugh, he folded his arms beneath his head. A dark flush highlighted his cheekbones as she laid her hand on his erection.

She wrapped her hand around it and moved it slightly, loving the velvety feel of him. His shoulders and neck rigid with tension, he groaned. "Tell me what you were thinking just now," she whispered, bending a little lower, her mouth an inch from the velvety tip of his erection.

When he didn't answer, she flicked her tongue over the erect tip. His abdomen under her hand hardened into a steel wall under immense pressure. Tension radiated from his every pore, the corded veins in his neck pulsing with life. "Is it simply that you don't care for body art?"

He shook his head.

She smiled, pleased with his answer. Her mouth wide-open, she took him into her mouth ever so slowly. A fierce rush of wetness gathered between her legs at his guttural moan. His hands crawled into hair. She pulled her mouth from him, licking every inch of the tight skin. "Do you not care for butterflies, then?"

He cursed as she blew at the soft head. "I have nothing against butterflies."

His words sounded far away, hoarse, drugged. She wrapped her hand around his erection again and moved it from base to the tip. A drop of moisture appeared at the rigid tip and she licked her lips in anticipation.

Their gazes collided, raw need mirrored in his. "Damn it, Liv. Take me into your mouth again."

His words were a command fueled by raw need, need that set something inside her on a fire. She licked the bead of moisture at the tip and moaned. He hardened a little more, if that was possible. "Give me something, Alexander, anything," she said, uncaring that her words were fueled by something far deeper than raw lust. And he knew it, because his mouth tightened into a line.

"Fine," she said, letting him go, even though every inch of her craved to stay.

He reached up and tugged her closer until her mouth was an inch from his. "You're a witch." His blue gaze blazed with an unknown emotion. "You want to know what I feel when I see your tattoo? *Jealousy*," he bit out. "For a minute, all I could think of was how many men had seen, touched and kissed that damn butterfly, like an uncivilized brute."

Olivia swallowed at the rawness in his tone. Her stomach clenched. She kissed the granite wall of his jaw, tugged his lower lip with her teeth. "I got it last month, so you're the first man to see it. I've wanted to get one for a long time, but I—"

She gasped as he pulled her on top of him and entered her. Arching her back, she felt pleasure like nothing she had felt before. Every inch of her skin tingled as they moved together to a wild rhythm, need spiraling higher and higher until she found release.

Alexander raised his hips and surged into her with a last fierce thrust. Her muscles tightened around him with contractions until release claimed him, too, an indescribable pleasure coupled with something else he couldn't recognize.

CHAPTER THIRTEEN

OLIVIA MOANED, HALF-ASLEEP, arousal seeping into her blood as a hot mouth glided over her tattoo and every inch of her back. She kept her eyes closed, breathing in the intimately erotic scent of Alexander and sex that lingered around them.

Her body ached, pleasantly, lethargic after he had kept her awake most of the night, after he had driven her to the edge and beyond so many times, drawing every inch of pleasure he could from her body.

Turning onto her back, she reached out her hand and hard muscles met her fingers. She ran it over his chest, lower and lower. His erection hardened, lengthened in her hand, and he bit her shoulder with a groan. The most exquisite thrill of power shuddered through her.

His hand snuck up to cover her breast, his mouth crushing her with his. She sunk her hands into his hair and hung on as his mouth moved lower over her jaw, to the pulse at her neck. She moaned as he licked the birthmark on the curve of her breast, the muscles in her lower belly tightening in anticipation.

She grumbled when he tugged her hand upward and kissed her palm. Opening her eyes, she looked into his blue eyes. He grinned, and Olivia felt the impact of his smile all the way to her toes. Need and a desperate longing to speak her mind, to say what she was thinking slammed her awake. She had never learned to how to keep things to herself, and she trembled now, struggling to contain the biggest truth of her life. She wanted to shout it, she wanted to revel in it.

"I don't want to stop," he whispered into her skin. "But if I have to leave for the Caribbean for a week, I have a lot of things to clear from my schedule."

"You are?" she mumbled, her hands stilling. She winced at the hint of dismay that crept into her voice.

He got out of the bed, tangling the sheets. Her pulse skyrocketed at the sight of his tight butt. "*We* are."

It took her a moment to pull her mind away from the muscled expanse of his back to what he had just said.

"I can't go Alexander, I…" She licked her lips as he, without an ounce of modesty, tugged his boxers and then his trousers up, all the while waiting for her to finish her thought. "My job, I…just spent two weeks in Paris. I can't take—"

"So bring work. I understand from Daniel that the budgeting has already been approved," he said, making dust of her excuse. He moved closer and pressed a kiss on her lips, a savage one that she felt all the way to her toes. "One week, Liv, after that we can go our—"

She kneeled on the bed and kissed him back, unwilling to let him finish the thought. With every kiss, every touch, she felt as if she was falling deeper and deeper into a hole that could close in on her any second. But goodbye, she couldn't say it already. Not just yet.

A smile curved his lips, lighting up the blues of his eyes. He pressed a kiss to her temple and tugged her out of the bed.

Standing on the other side of the bed, she dressed and threw some clothes into an overnight bag while he padded the small space of her apartment, glued to his cell, no doubt canceling his numerous engagements.

As she maneuvered past him to get to the coffeemaker, he grinned, his phone still on. She yelped when he grabbed her wrist and pulled her to him. His body against hers was a haven of warmth, a promise of pleasure. But it was his arms around her, his boyish smile as he kissed her that clawed at her.

She wanted to turn around and hug him, she wanted to breathe the words that were clamoring inside her into his skin. But of course, she couldn't. And she had just signed up for a week of this torment.

As he picked up her bag and opened the door, she looked back. "Wait, I can't leave like this. You broke the lock."

He grinned. "Already taken care of. By the time we come back, Carlos will arrange for someone to move all your stuff to a new apartment."

"New apartment? Alexander, I can't afford it and I don't want your—"

"I knew you would say that. But you're forgetting that you just landed a new contract for your agency. You'll get a pay raise—"

"Don't do this, Alexander. I mean it, stay out of my..."

For an infinitesimal second, the smile slipped from his face, and his jaw clamped down. She reached him and cupped his jaw. If a week was all he was going to give her, she didn't want to spend it fighting with him. "I know you think I need someone to take care of me. But I don't, okay? I couldn't bear it if anyone...repeated or even speculated like that reporter. I—"

He nodded and kissed her into silence in the dimly lit corridor. She laughed as he drew back with a groan. "The sooner I get you on the plane, the sooner I can ravish you all over again."

His words sent tingles over her skin. Within minutes,

they were standing in front of her building. Dawn was just a few minutes away, and it streaked the sky orange. She shivered and pulled the lapels of her thin sweatshirt together and made a face at him.

He pulled her into the warmth of his arms and checked the silver Rolex on his wrist. "Carlos will be here any minute and then we'll be off."

She made a face like a petulant child. "I don't understand why we have to leave so early."

"This way, we can leave before the wolves are out, before there's even a chance of anyone—"

She paled at his words and he tugged her even closer, forcing her to look at him. "I'm sorry, I wish there wasn't any need to skulk around like this, I wish I could… But with things the way they are, I don't want to risk anything. You understand that, don't you?"

Olivia nodded and burrowed into him, striving to compose herself, to keep the misery crawling up her throat locked tight. Here she was again, scuttling in the dark with a lover…

Was she being selfish if she wanted an open relationship? One where she could just be herself, one where she could shout to the world that someone as honorable as Alexander wanted to be with her?

What was she doing? Why was she prolonging the moment of utter agony? Was she really stupid enough to hope that something would change in a week? That Alexander would suddenly open up himself to what he felt about her?

Her stomach fell endlessly at the thought of never seeing him again, never touching him.

With every breath in her she wanted to go, she wanted to steal the week with him. But how could she settle for something less than she deserved? And this time, she wasn't naive, stupid to believe that if she just went along, if she did everything right, maybe, then maybe her love would be returned.

Alexander was never going to change his mind, never going to give things between them a chance.

He had shown her everything she could be, everything she already was and he would walk away without a backward glance. Her stomach became a mass of pain. She wanted to cry, rage at him, at herself.

And as much as she wished, she couldn't revert back to type, she couldn't reverse the knowledge that she deserved better.

She couldn't deceive herself, even for him.

"Alexander." She clasped the granite jaw with her hands, forcing the words past her throat, her body trembling with pain. Pain at what she was going to do. "I can't do this, I can't go with you."

Olivia's words were barely a whisper, yet it shook everything within Alexander.

"Look at me," he said, frustration coursing through him. Why couldn't she, for once, do as he said without argument?

He thought she would resist but she didn't. Her face was pale, and a sheen of tears glimmered in her gaze that knocked the breath out of him. "Damn it, Liv."

"You know what I'm going to say, don't you?"

He looked into her beautiful brown eyes, and the depth of emotion in hers sent a cold chill over his skin. His stomach churned with a viciousness he couldn't stop. He moved his finger to her mouth, but she pushed it away and dropped a kiss into his palm. Because when had anything stopped Olivia?

She wrapped her hand around his face and kissed him, the press of her lips against his soft and warm. A tiny smile, full of emotion curved her mouth. "I'm in love with you."

There was no recrimination in those words, no anguish, just simple acceptance. Yet they dealt a blow to his solar plexus, leaving him winded, battered. He pulled his hands from her face. What could he say to her? He'd come back, he'd stayed last night knowing that it was wrong. "Don't do this, Liv. Don't push this on me. I told you—"

"I don't want anything from you. Don't you get it? I love you despite knowing that you'll never admit to feeling something for me, knowing that you'll never give us a chance, that at the end of this week, you'll wipe me from your mind. I can't help how I feel. I wish I could change that, I want to shut it down like you do because it hurts so much. But I am what I am."

In the back of his mind, he'd known all along it would come to this. Olivia did nothing in half measures, her heart engaged in everything she did. Yet he'd ignored what he'd known, because he'd been weak. And now he was going to break her heart.

He felt like the lowest scum on earth. He wrenched the words from somewhere deep within, a place where he didn't want to look at again. He turned away from her. "I have nothing to give you, Liv."

Her hands crept over his shoulder, kneading and pressing the muscles there. An all-too-familiar hunger rose in his belly as she pressed her forehead against his nape and kissed him. "You really don't think it works like that, do you? There's no way out of this for me." Her hands wrapped around him, she pressed herself to him. Everything within him quaked, his gut clenched, rebelled.

Her hug said it all, everything she was—giving, open— and everything he had trained himself to not want, to not need.

"You're so bent on not letting anything Isabella did to you linger, don't you see you're letting her win, letting her influence how you live your life?"

"That's not going to work on me." He stiffened. It felt like needles had clawed under his skin, making every word hard to say, but he pushed it out. "I don't want this, Olivia. I don't want to feel anything, I can't take it."

Anger flashed in her gaze. She pushed away his hands and wiped the tears from her face. "Then, leave now, when I still have the strength to push you away."

He wanted to argue, he wanted to shove her words from his mind. He dropped a kiss to her forehead and wrapped his arms around her. He crushed her mouth with his, her soft moan rumbling inside him. He couldn't help himself. He'd already fallen in his own eyes, so what did it matter?

He bent and kissed the pulse drumming at her neck, knowing that it would drive her crazy. Her moan fueled him, bringing down the last ounce of sanity within him.

Something prickled at his nape, and he turned to the other side. A flash went on, a flare of light in the dark of dawn, blinding him.

Fury pumped through him and he turned to shield Liv with his body, but it was too late. A rabid look in his eyes, the reporter clicked a few more times and then disappeared into the dark, before Alexander could even move. His reflexes were slow, as though his mind couldn't comprehend the horror of what had happened.

Silence had never seemed so deafening, so cold that his skin prickled. He felt her hand on his shoulder but he didn't turn. If he did, he didn't know what he would do. He swallowed past the mass of fury thrashing in his throat. He raked his hand through his hair, tension vibrating through every inch of him. His hands shook, his muscles burned with fury.

He cursed, even though it did nothing to alleviate the fury coursing through him. Guilt coiled through him, gaining a foothold over his insides. *He was responsible for this.*

He should've never forgotten her struggle yesterday

with the paparazzi. He had stayed knowing he was putting everything he'd worked for over the past twelve years at risk and he'd done it, anyway.

He had lost control, he had given in and he was going to pay the price.

"Go back inside, Olivia. And stay there."

He turned toward the street and walked to the approaching car. At the car, he barked out instructions to Carlos to locate the reporter. Even then, the need to turn back, the need to kiss her was an ache in his gut. But he couldn't.

Giving into his emotions had only created a mess he had no one but himself to blame for. He had to do damage control, he had to make sure his sister was safe. He had to prepare himself for the battle that was going to come from his mother.

Only there was no shutting away the words Olivia had spoken so freely.

Olivia couldn't think, couldn't move for a moment. She had stood frozen, her hands wrapped around herself, a chill overtaking her with each passing second. A shiver had inched its way up her spine and she'd shaken uncontrollably as she'd realized the truth. Alexander wasn't coming back.

A cry tore from her throat as she sank to her bed, tears pooling in her eyes. It was over.

She had no idea how long she lay in a heap like that. The darkness of dawn gave way to morning. Sunlight filtered through the small window. Feeling as if there was lead in her veins instead of blood, she sat up as her phone chirped.

"Where are you?" Kim's concerned voice rang through the phone.

Wiping her face, Olivia straightened. She swallowed the misery clawing to break through. She needed to tell Kim before she found out from that tabloid, before anyone else did. "I'm home, why?"

"Oh, Liv. Why didn't you tell me? You just stay there, okay?"

Unease crept up Olivia's spine. "Wait, Kim. I need to tell you something…about Alexander and me. I…."

"God, Liv. I know." Kim's voice vibrated over the phone.

Olivia flinched. "No, Kim. Please listen to me. I would never hurt you…please believe me. I fell in…" Her words piled on top of each other. "It was only after—"

"I know that. I know that you would never do anything to hurt me. I mean, I was the one who dragged you into this whole mess." Kim sounded tortured, pained, her voice quaking. "And now, they're calling you…whatever you do, just wait in your apartment, okay. Just stay put."

Before she could reply that she had no wish to leave, Kim hung up. Olivia sat up and only then did the small noises filter through to her brain. Footsteps shuffling outside her door, a low hum of whispers creeping in through the window… Pushing her hair out of the way, she went to it.

And jumped back as though someone had stuck a hot poker through the window.

Swarms of sleazy tabloid reporters, and more than one local network news crew were parked in front of her building. Sweat beaded on her lip, her leg muscles cramped up. It felt as if her worst nightmare had opened up shop in front of her building, ready to swallow her up.

This couldn't be happening again, not to her… She had done nothing to deserve it this time, nothing but fall in love….

She bent over and forced herself to breathe, tears streaming down her face. Now she understood why Kim had sounded concerned. She knew it in the back of her mind, she had known it was bad that she had been photographed with Alexander, kissing him, in his arms.

But until now, the reality of what it meant hadn't sunk in. How could it when all she could think of, all she could see was Alexander's face, anger and disgust vying on it, all she felt was the crushing pain that he could walk away? Her stomach fell as the haze of grief cleared and more and more things scrambled into her head.

Scandal...Emily, Isabella.

She couldn't let Emily pay the price for her mistake. Not because she hadn't been strong enough to say no to Alexander. Not because he refused to take a chance on them.

She stood up and scrubbed her face. Every instinct in her screamed at her to lie low, to curl up in her bed and not step outside the apartment.

Fear was a tight knot in her stomach. The more it clawed at her, the faster she moved. She dressed quickly, grabbed her handbag, put her sunglasses on and closed the door behind her.

Within minutes, she was pushing through the rusty metal door in the foyer and stepping onto the pavement.

The uproar of the small crowd, the stench of their curiosity knocked her in the gut, and she almost slipped.

Taking even a breath felt like work, but she did it. She faltered before catching the newspaper thrown at her with the image of Alexander and her kissing on the front page. They looked lost in each other, lost to the world.

Olivia Stanton's Latest Conquest: Her Twin's Husband.

The headline ripped through her, and she gasped for breath, as though a knife had been plunged into her heart.

Cameras clicked, microphones were thrust in her face, but she kept moving, not focusing on any of them, letting all their images shift and blur, struggling to let their invasive, soul-crushing questions slide by her.

"Does your sister know what you did, Olivia?"

"Is he sleeping with both of you?"

"What is about another woman's man that draws you so much?"

She held it together, she walked past them and miraculously, almost made it to a waiting cab. Until someone shouted the worst question at her, the one that tore through her, the one that almost knuckled her down right there.

"Do you think he's in love with you?"

A few of the worst hours of her life later, Olivia reached Kim's apartment complex in an upscale neighborhood of Manhattan. Thankfully, there were no reporters hovering on the street. But she knew it was only a matter of time before they descended on Kim. With hurried steps, she walked through the door held open by the uniformed doorman, his prying gaze eating her up.

All she wanted to do was to jump in the shower, get into bed and not emerge for a few days. She pressed the up arrow for the elevator and the doors opened with a smooth swish.

And her father stepped out.

She froze. Her gut clenched tight into a painful, unforgiving knot. The muscles in her legs tightened. The urge to flee pummeled her blood. She threw a quick look behind her, trying to see past the foyer into the street, weighing the chance of leaving without someone from the press trailing her again.

"Yes, run away again. It's not like you're capable of anything else. You were always like your mother."

The words landed on her like the sharp points of countless needles, flaying her. And still, all she wanted was to do exactly as he said. *Run away.*

Her hands hung by her sides, she turned around and forced herself to meet his gaze.

Silver hair cut short, he was immaculately dressed in a

gray suit, his favorite pair of platinum cuff links gleaming at the cuffs, the pair that she had always wanted to pound to dust with a hammer. "Hello, Dad," she said, the words incredibly hard to form. She swallowed past the fear scratching her throat. She didn't want to explain, but this time, she needed to. She knew how bad it looked. She shouldn't care, but she couldn't let him go on believing the absolute worst about her. "I know how it looks, but —"

"Have you no shame, Olivia?" His words boomed around the empty corridor, echoing around her, until all she could hear was the derision etched into each of them. Her skin crawled. "I knew it. You're nothing better than a slut who would betray her own twin. Have you fallen so low that only a married man would do?"

She moved her hands to her ears, trembling, each word sinking its claws into her skin. "Stop it, Dad. Give me a chance to—"

"No wonder you were successful with that advertising contract."

She tried to breathe through the crushing pain in her chest. It shouldn't come as a surprise, his words shouldn't have this much power to hurt her, yet they did. "That's not true. I worked hard for—"

"Do you expect me to believe that? That you achieved anything through hard work and talent? The only thing you were ever good at was making a shameless spectacle of yourself with any man who would look at you twice."

"How could I be good at anything? You constantly pushed me into things I didn't want to do, criticized anything I did enjoy. You leeched away every ounce of joy from my life, you belittled me until…"

Alexander's words came back to her. Wrong careers, wrong men, she had pursued all the wrong things just because she hadn't thought any better of herself. Because inside where it mattered, she hadn't thought herself worthy of anything, that she would never be good enough for someone nice and decent.

Like Alexander.

Familiar pain scratched her insides, but something else fueled her, too. She *was* better than she thought, she did deserve better and she had already proved it to herself.

It had hurt like a part of her was being wrenched away, but she had walked away from Alexander, she had stood up for what she was worth. Her heart might never recover from it, she would never stop loving him, but she had nothing to prove to anyone, either, least of all her father.

She took a couple of steps toward him. She hadn't stood this close to him in a while, the smell of the cigars he enjoyed swathed her, bittersweet in the memories it evoked. "Kim—" she didn't want to betray her sister's news "—she knows about us and she doesn't care. And Alexander, he… cares about me—"

"Don't add delusion to your already long list of weaknesses. The truth is, a man like Alexander will kick you to the curb the minute his fancy wears off, and he has, hasn't he?"

It was the worst she had believed about herself, and hearing the words from her father's mouth ate into her newfound beliefs. It was so easy, too easy to stop fighting his words, to let the old fears creep back in, to think that Alexander had walked away so easily because it had been *her.* That she hadn't been enough, her love hadn't been enough.

No. She took a deep breath. She wasn't going to do this to herself anymore.

The wall of hurt she had nursed since childhood splintered, the wall she had cowered behind, a fierce rush of anger breaking through. "The truth? The truth is that you're a bully, and nothing more." She breathed hard, feeling as though her lungs would collapse, as though the pain tightening her stomach would never ease. "You drove Mom away with your constant degrading, you made me think so little of myself and Kim, *God*, you made her believe she was worth nothing if she didn't excel at everything. You're a vile man who draws satisfaction from belittling everyone around you. And I hope I never see you again."

Her shoulders stiff, her head held high, she walked into the elevator and hit the up arrow. Every muscle in her body trembled, every nerve stretched so tight that she felt as if she would break if she even took a breath. Tears streamed down her face. She slid to a heap on the floor as the elevator moved up. But she didn't care.

She hadn't cowered in front of her father.

She hoped she never saw him again in this lifetime. Like walking away from Alexander, she didn't have it in her to do it twice.

CHAPTER FOURTEEN

ALEXANDER SWITCHED ON the flat-screen monitor in his office, and halted. Olivia's smiling face filled the forty-two inch monitor. His heart jumped into his throat. It was a shot from when she had starred in the reality dating show, which hadn't ended well for her.

Her head thrown back, she was laughing at something her date said. Her eyes shone with brilliance, the wide curve of her mouth sent his heart pulsing. The screen flicked back to the anchor and he muted it, his stomach churning viciously. He'd heard the sensational story for three days and had no wish to hear it again.

But Olivia was a survivor. Any other woman would have long ago given up, her life a combination of impulses, bad luck and all the wrong people. But she hadn't. Every time something had brought her down, she had dusted herself off and fought back. And she had finally found success in advertising. Except he had ruined it all. Now, even the contract she had won was tainted, reduced into something cheap and tawdry because of him.

It had been three of the worst days of his life. Everything he had known, everything he had built, had unraveled around him as the scandal hit the media Friday afternoon. By that time, he had taken all the measures he could, made sure Emily was in sight. Except the one thing he should have done.

By the time he'd recovered from the shock of what he'd brought on himself, hours had passed. He'd dispatched Carlos to pick up Olivia, to take her to a safe place, but he'd been too late.

Olivia, being Olivia, had stepped out into the horde of overzealous reporters lined up along her street. The shot zeroed in on her face as she ventured past the microphones and cameras. The invasive questions, the allegations of their affair, they had pecked at her like a pack of hungry vultures.

Why? Why hadn't she just stayed at her apartment? He knew how much she feared them. And yet she had walked into the throng.

A hand fisted his heart, making it hard to breathe as pictures of him and Olivia filled the screen. They looked lost in each other, his hands on her waist, their bodies glued to each other.

Nausea rose inside him and he turned it off, unable to stand it any longer. It wasn't enough that Alexander himself was castigated, his background, the story of his parents, everything brought into the foreground to illuminate the scandal, to portray that he was finally, a man who made mistakes like everyone else.

No, Olivia was paying the highest price of them all.

If he was attacked, it was nothing compared to what the media called her—the woman who'd been having an affair with her twin's husband. As if he had no part in the whole thing, as if it was all her fault. They'd shredded her to pieces and the unfairness of it burned a path of fury through him.

While in reality, she wasn't at fault at all. She had never lied to him, never shied away from what she was, what she felt. And everything she'd given him had been reduced to a tawdry affair because of him. He had become one of the numerous people who had hurt her.

Emotions roiled through him like lava, anger at himself, frustration and the worst of all, guilt. It clawed up his insides. He had not only brought the worst to her, but he had left her alone to deal with it. He had been so intent on running from what she made him feel, he had become a man with no honor, a man who would leave the woman who had done nothing but stand by him, to the wolves.

And it hurt. Whatever he did, however he thought about it, the pain wouldn't go away. He wanted to make it go away. He wanted to shut off everything and go back. It was as though everything he'd always been able to control was rebelling, drowning him in it.

He had everything under control. He had a team of the best lawyers in the country to take on anything his mother threw at him. Yes, his company had lost some of its share value thanks to the scandal, but he had enough money that nothing was unrecoverable.

Then why did he feel so empty and weighed down? He'd restored his world to normality, but that sense of control that had always been his strength couldn't shake off the void.

He grabbed the paperweight from his table and chucked it with all the force he could muster. An action he would have laughed at as juvenile, something he would've never done a month ago. The wall caved slightly under the impact, and he turned away to the French windows that revealed an uncommonly gray New York. He stood looking into the city, letting the cold creep into his skin.

Had she finally washed her hands off him, given up on him? Had she finally realized what a coward he was?

He stared at his image in the glass. Outwardly, nothing was different. But everything had changed inside. He let the truth he'd been fighting in, let it seep into his blood, sink into his cells.

He had thrown away the best thing that had happened to him because he was a damn coward, too scared to feel, too scared to take what he had wanted all his life.

He missed Olivia with a longing he had never felt before. It was a constant ache in his gut, a fist in his chest. He missed her mischievous laugh, he missed the way she challenged everything he said, he missed the way she didn't let him get away with anything.

After everything he'd gone through the past few days, after everything he'd felt, he'd thought he was done. Only a tendril of fear curled itself around his heart now, stealing his breath, drenching him in a chill that had nothing to do with the temperature.

He, Alexander King, the man who had made millions through sheer will, the man who'd arranged everything in his life to suit him was scared that he was too late, that he'd lost the one woman who'd looked beyond the surface, the one woman who'd smashed through his barriers and made him feel something.

And this time, he didn't even have the hope of picking himself up from this, because Olivia had gouged a hole in him, had wrenched a part of him away.

He was that seventeen-year-old boy again, hurting like hell, drowning in pain, mired in guilt.

He turned as the door opened. Carlos walked in, his expression revealing nothing. Before Alex could question him, the door opened a little more and in walked his mother. He had known this was coming, he'd been prepared for it. Yet it pulled at something inside him and he had no strength or control left to push it away.

"Hello, Isabella," he murmured, tucking his hands into the pockets of his trousers. His mother looked stunning as ever. "Wise choice, not to bring Nick along. At least you will get a civil conversation out of me."

She said nothing, only stared at him, her brown gaze raking over him.

He poured himself a drink and settled into the leather sofa in the adjoining lounge. "Could you just not resist the temptation to see me at my lowest?" The bitterness in his voice surprised even him.

Isabella stared at him warily, as though she was afraid he would just lose it. And the way he was feeling, she wasn't far from truth. "Are you at your lowest?"

He stared into his drink, uncaring of what he revealed. "Yes. So, whatever you've come to do, do it fast and get out."

She sat down on the couch, her beautiful face level with his. "I'm not your enemy, Alexander." Two weeks ago, he could have crushed the pang that ran through him, he wouldn't even have registered the note of concern that crept into her voice. It was a measure of how much had changed in his perception because of Olivia and it staggered him.

He studied her, the anger, the resentment he had felt so long ago seeping into him unchecked. His hand trembled as he took a sip. "You want to take Emily from me."

She shook her head. "No, I don't. I know it's hard for you to believe but your father and I are different people now."

He snorted, Olivia's claim that people could change running through his head.

"I don't want to drag you through a court battle. All I want is to see Emily and...*you*. I was getting desperate, yes... But...Olivia convinced me not to do anything rash."

He bolted from the couch and dropped his glass on the coffee table. The drink sloshed over it and onto the thick the most but fear stopped him. It felt as if his whole life was hanging by a thread, and it scared the hell out of him to bare it all in front of her. "I wanted to thank you for what you did for Emily. Isabella said she wasn't going to sue and I told her she could see Emily."

Olivia smiled through the tears pooling in her eyes. She wanted to throw her arms around him and hold on for as long as she could, so much that it was a physical ache in her stomach. "I didn't do it just for her. I did it for you."

He tugged her toward him, his palms moving up and down her arms. "For me?"

"I didn't want that tiny part of you that still feels something to be crushed completely. Because that's what would have happened if Isabella sued you. You would have closed yourself off." And she wouldn't have been able to reach him in this lifetime. Because the hope that he would change his mind if not now, then sometime in the future, was the only thing that was keeping her going. Really it had been a purely selfish move on her part.

His gaze filled with such tenderness, such humility that Olivia wanted to hug him and kiss him. She even jerked up from the bed, only to fall back on her knees. She couldn't bear it if he pushed her away again.

"Don't do that, Liv. Don't give up on me now," he said, his words vibrating with pain. "I've been going out of my mind for three days," he said, moving his mouth to her temple, breathing his words into her skin.

She hugged herself, feeling frayed along the edges, battered, as if a wound she'd thought healed kept opening again and again. "You can't do this. You can't just come back into my life whenever you want, dictate your own set of rules and then walk away. I won't let you. I won't let you take away what little I have left."

He tugged her hands into his. "No, I know. I promised myself I wouldn't even touch you until I said what I want to." His voice was gruff. "I have never let myself feel so much that it's a giant ball of ache in my gut. And a part of me flinches and just wants to shut down. I want to do this, I want to tell you how I feel but opening up myself, it's the scariest thing I've done since I walked out on my parents."

His eyelids flickered down for a second, hiding his expression from her. He touched his forehead to hers, and sighed. "I'm in love with you, Liv, and it terrifies the hell out of me. I missed you so much that there should be a gaping hole inside me. I need you to tell me that I haven't blown my chance with you, that you haven't given up on me."

"I do love you, Alexander. Nothing in this world is going to change that."

His heart beat normally for the first time in three days. "Will you forgive me for leaving you like that?"

A soft smile curved her mouth. "You're forgiven," she said quietly.

He couldn't go another moment without touching her, without kissing her. He pulled her up for a thorough kiss that breathed new life into his blood. He didn't want to wait another minute to make her his. His heart felt too big for the excitement drumming through him.

He shifted her hair from her shoulder and pressed a kiss. "Will you marry me, Olivia?"

Her quiet smile slipped. He turned her toward him, uncertainty skewering him. "I don't have a ring because I know you hate diamonds."

Olivia took a deep breath, hating what she had to say. "I—"

A shadow loomed over Alexander's face. He ran a hand over his nape, his mouth a rigid line of pain. "So you *have* changed your mind."

She scooted from his lap, to the edge of the bed. She cupped his jaw and held fast as he tried to move away. "I want to be with you so much that it's a constant ache in my heart, Alexander," she said, pulling his hand to her heart which thundered at his touch. "But these past three days, they have made me doubt everything."

His heart squeezed up with pain, Alexander took a step back. "I know I hurt you—"

"It's not what you did, Alexander. All the women you have dated before me, they were all perfect like Kim, without a blemish." She laid her palm on his mouth and hid her face in his shirt. "If this whole circus with the media has taught me anything, it's that they will always haunt you, always be hungry for a story about you. They will keep digging, keep making stories. Even if they extinguish every angle of my past, what about our future? I'm someone who will always make mistakes, who can never be perfect. Only one day the disdain will be back in your eyes again, and it will absolutely crush me. If you begin to hate me again, I'll break, Alexander. And you will, *eventually.*"

Alexander pulled Olivia up and hugged her to him until neither of them could breathe with the pressure. He wanted to touch her soft curves, lose himself in her until she agreed to anything he asked, but he fought the urge to do that. She trembled in his arms and he pressed a kiss to her shoulder. "I'm not saying everything will be a bed of roses, Liv. There will be days when you will want to kill me as surely as there will be days when I'll want to tie you up so that you can't wreak havoc on us. But, your past, that will never bother me. It's what made you the woman you are today. And it's that woman I love, strengths and faults."

A shadow still diluted her smile. "But don't you want to take this slow, play boyfriend-girlfriend for a little while before—"

"No. I want the whole world to know that you're my wife, my equal. We'll learn our way as we go. The most important thing you've taught me is that life can't be lived

in a vacuum, that you have to keep taking chances on yourself even if it means you might get hurt. So we'll fail and
we'll try again. It is the scariest thing I've ever wanted to
do, but I want to do it with you. I want to laugh with you,
take care of you, grow old with you, even if it also means
you'll drive me up the wall every other day."

She met his gaze, a glimmer of a smile in it. "You really
think so?"

He laughed and pushed her back into the bed. He tugged
his shirt out of his trousers with hurried movements and
slid into the bed next to her. Ignoring her gasp, he pulled
her tee up in one movement. Desire was a low hum in his
blood as he gazed at her tight-tipped breasts, the indent of
her navel and her pink panties with little bows begging to
be ripped. He bent his head and licked a wet path around
her cute navel. "Yes and you better be prepared. I can't
wait for everyone to know that Olivia Stanton's generous
heart, amazing spirit and her luscious body belong to me
and only me," he said, struggling to hide the possessiveness that bled into his words. The emotion he felt for her
choked and terrified him with its strength. One day at a
time, like he had told her, one day at a time. "If there's one
thing you should know about this, it's that there's no half-
ways about this, Liv. I'm never going to let you go, ever."

Olivia plunged her hands into his hair and pulled his
head up, every inch of her writing with pleasure. The
possessiveness in his gaze, in his words, rolled over her
skin. She kissed him with an urgency that had her suck
and bite his lower lip.

He laughed and stroked her thighs, his fingers inching
toward her core, achy and throbbing for his touch. "Not
that you have a choice except to agree," he said, his voice
dark and hoarse.

Olivia raised a brow. "No?"

"Not if you want me to do all the wicked things I want to

do to you." His hands parted her legs, stole under her panties and his thumb flicked at the heat between her thighs. She closed her eyes and moaned, pushing herself into his touch. "So is it a yes?"

She opened her eyes, and gazed at him. Love and desire gazed back at her, washing away her doubts. "Yes," she whispered. He plunged a finger into her core and rubbed at her swollen folds again. Olivia laughed and gave into the sensation piling upon her, whispering the single word over and over again as Alexander took her to ecstasy.

* * * * *

#3189 A DANGEROUS SOLACE
by Lucy Ellis

Gianluca Benedetti might not initially recognize Ava Lord, but the memories soon come rushing back! Exploring their reignited passion, Ava realizes the danger of opening her heart, as the closer he gets, the more cracks in her armor appear....

#3190 SECRETS OF A POWERFUL MAN
The Bond of Brothers
by Chantelle Shaw

Salvatore Castallano is haunted by the accident that left a blank in his memory. His young daughter is the one bright light in his dark existence. He'll do anything for her...even move Darcey Rivers—a delicious temptation—into his castle!

#3191 VISCONTI'S FORGOTTEN HEIR
by Elizabeth Power

Magenta is finally on track after suffering from amnesia. But, meeting Andreas Visconti's familiar gaze, she *knows* he's the father of her child! It's crucial she decipher the scattered puzzle of her mind and recall more than just memories of his touch....

#3192 A TOUCH OF TEMPTATION
The Sensational Stanton Sisters
by Tara Pammi

CEO Kimberly Stanton has rocked the international business world with the announcement of her marriage to outrageous Brazilian bad-boy tycoon Diego Pereira, *and* a pregnancy! If salacious rumors are already spreading, who can say what lies ahead for society's most notorious couple?

REQUEST YOUR FREE BOOKS!

HARLEQUIN® *Presents®*

PASSION GUARANTEED SEDUCTION

2 FREE NOVELS PLUS
2 FREE GIFTS!

YES! Please send me 2 FREE Harlequin Presents® novels and my 2 FREE gifts (gifts are worth about $10). After receiving them, if I don't wish to receive any more books, I can return the shipping statement marked "cancel." If I don't cancel, I will receive 6 brand-new novels every month and be billed just $4.30 per book in the U.S. or $4.99 per book in Canada. That's a saving of at least 14% off the cover price! It's quite a bargain! Shipping and handling is just 50¢ per book in the U.S. and 75¢ per book in Canada.* I understand that accepting the 2 free books and gifts places me under no obligation to buy anything. I can always return a shipment and cancel at any time. Even if I never buy another book, the two free books and gifts are mine to keep forever.

106/306 HDN FVRK

Name _____ (PLEASE PRINT)

Address _____ Apt. #

City _____ State/Prov. _____ Zip/Postal Code

Signature (if under 18, a parent or guardian must sign)

Mail to the **Harlequin® Reader Service:**
IN U.S.A.: P.O. Box 1867, Buffalo, NY 14240-1867
IN CANADA: P.O. Box 609, Fort Erie, Ontario L2A 5X3

**Are you a current subscriber to Harlequin Presents books
and want to receive the larger-print edition?
Call 1-800-873-8635 or visit www.ReaderService.com.**

* Terms and prices subject to change without notice. Prices do not include applicable taxes. Sales tax applicable in N.Y. Canadian residents will be charged applicable taxes. Offer not valid in Quebec. This offer is limited to one order per household. Not valid for current subscribers to Harlequin Presents books. All orders subject to credit approval. Credit or debit balances in a customer's account(s) may be offset by any other outstanding balance owed by or to the customer. Please allow 4 to 6 weeks for delivery. Offer available while quantities last.

Your Privacy—The Harlequin® Reader Service is committed to protecting your privacy. Our Privacy Policy is available online at www.ReaderService.com or upon request from the Harlequin Reader Service.

We make a portion of our mailing list available to reputable third parties that offer products we believe may interest you. If you prefer that we not exchange your name with third parties, or if you wish to clarify or modify your communication preferences, please visit us at www.ReaderService.com/consumerchoice or write to us at Harlequin Reader Service Preference Service, P.O. Box 9062, Buffalo, NY 14269. Include your complete name and address.

HPI3